Clocktower Books, San Diego

Dystopia USA 2049

By

John Argo

Publisher: Clocktower Books
www.clocktowerbooks.com
P.O. Box 600973 Grantville Station
San Diego, California 92160-0973
e-mail: editorial@clocktowerbooks.com

Track 01. UFO Ambush

Stakeout –
Night Desert

1. Desert Stakeout

Joe Mackinson was on stakeout in an unmarked DEA car, at a desert oasis outside San Diego at night, thinking about Carly and the tuna fish salad she'd made for him, when he noticed a flash overhead. Shooting star, he thought—the desert air was filled with them some nights, especially when the air was cold and clear like this. He heard a distant pop, and listened carefully, but heard nothing more but the wind sighing over the desert floor and through the river reeds near his car.

A faraway coyote called to its hunting partners, and an owl screeched closer by. Nothing more.

The desert itself seemed luminescent, under the incredible carpet of stars in the black sky. Mack had parked on a dark road, under riverside trees. He was waiting for a group of Sonoran narco-traffickers to drive past on their way to meet their Tijuana equivalents for a twenty million dollar cocaine deal. DEA had an inside man, who somehow managed to stay alive and send out valuable information.

Mack sighed. What could go wrong tonight? What couldn't go wrong? For the moment, his life was quiet. Often, meetings like this ended up in a shoot-out, and the Mexican cartels were among the most cruel and vicious thugs in the world. Mack had traded fire with some of them in other border regions, and he'd seen what happens when you put a human being in a barrel of gasoline and toss in a match, as had recently happened to a DEA informant in Juarez.

Still, Mack was passionate about his job. He didn't love it. He loved his wife, not his job. That's how he saw it. He was addicted to the excitement, the urgent sense of doing something worthwhile. Sometimes it was terrifying. He had a bullet scar in his arm, a knife scar along his ribs, a very faint razor scar on his left cheek (after plastic surgery), and shrapnel in one leg to show for his eight years in the department. Carly worried about him all the time. He kept promising he was ready for a desk job, but he always put off the paperwork.

As he sat waiting for the radio call for action from his boss, he unscrewed a steel thermos. Suddenly, the crappy car smelled like their kitchen in the Talmadge section of Mid-City San Diego. As frogs chirruped a chorus in a stream buried in willows and reeds to one side of the dirt path, Special Agent Joseph Mackinson unwrapped the lunch Carly had packed for him.

The night was cool, in contrast to the day's desert heat earlier. The night was moonless, and there was fog on the river below. It was too dark, so he turned on the book light next to the computer. The hooded lamp cast a tiny spot of light on the brown paper bag. It was a tidy little package, as she would make with her even fingers with their dark red nail gloss. He smiled to himself, picturing her—straight dark-brown hair swinging in a page boy cut, lively blue eyes, a businesslike pout of rouged lips. There was a perfectly made tuna salad sandwich, on toast, with the edges cut off, a pickle on the side, a small bag of chips, and a dark red apple the color of her fingernails. What he wouldn't give to be home with her, rather than sitting in this godforsaken foggy swamp, hoping to tail a gang of murderers to a nest full with more murderers...

Somewhere, a barely audible noise rose up that didn't sound natural. He wasn't ready to notice it yet, other than to start becoming faintly aware that something had changed.

Something was changing around him. The awareness had just begun to nibble at his consciousness, but he wasn't ready to pay attention to it.

As he bit off a corner of the sandwich and started to chew— crisp bits of celery killing the fishy taste of the tuna, getting the seafood-love from Carly, a grin and a wink from the kitchen where he'd rather be with her than this godforsaken hole in the middle of nowhere—he heard a thump.

He stopped chewing and listened, with a big tasty blob in his mouth. He caught a glimpse of himself in the rearview mirror—a slightly scared looking white guy about 30, with a light brown buzz cut and a desert camo uniform.

He heard two more distinct thumping sounds somewhere behind him.

As he bit off another piece of bread and tuna, he used his free hand to surreptitiously make sure the doors were locked. The windows were slightly open, an inch or two, and he left them like that for air circulation.

He shifted the sandwich to his other hand, and checked on the seat to his right. There lay his 9 mm Glock in its canvas holster, and several full clips on the sprawling belt. An Uzi lay on the floor on the front passenger side. The windows were ordinary safety glass, but the doors and body were of the new bathtub kind, with a poured, lightweight composite interior that could absorb most ordinary ammunition, or at least slow it down if fired from ambush.

He had a partner, Leonard 'Leo' Roberts, clean-cut young Black guy from Florida, age 28, with two years in the agency. Leo had called at the last minute to say he had a flat and would be late. He'd ride in with the rest of the team, and join Mack once the pursuit got rolling.

There was a louder thump.

Wind shoved against the car.

It was a slight motion, but an abrupt little jerk that made hackles rise along Mack's spine.

It was accompanied by a tiny sigh or a gust of wind outside, or maybe a moan of pain or fright.

"Okay, what's going on?" he muttered to himself. He killed the reading light and turned off the little fan humming on the dashboard.

Holding the sandwich in his left, he brought the Glock over his chest with his right.

He laid the heavy gun in his lap.

He slowly and quietly clicked himself free of the seatbelt, which he let roll away over his shoulder.

He picked up the gun and held it flat against his chest with his index finger resting on the trigger guard. For about half a minute he held his breath and listened intently.

The faintest of breezes stirred the long, hanging willow branches. Here, out near Ocotillo Wells, several miles north of Interstate 8, there was almost no man-made light pollution. If he were to step from the car, and walk about 200 feet up the shrouded, corridor-like road under the tree canopy, he'd be on a dirt road in the desert, looking up at a collection of stars as rich as a carpet of diamonds.

Sometimes, on a night like this, it was hard to make out the grand wheel of the Milky Way because there were so many lights in the sky. But he wasn't about to leave the radio, since a call from the boss about Carlos Ochoa and his gang was due at any time. Even here in the dark, there was a glow, a Gegenschein, of starlight that almost made leaves of the massive river oaks look as if they had snow on them.

He took another bite and started chewing. Damn, he wanted this sandwich. His stomach was in knots with hunger, and that coffee smelled roasted and good, black and crisp.

He heard two thumps in succession, and a low gust of wind moaned past the car, buffeting it.

No mistake now. Something was going on. Were the Ochoa gangsters playing tricks with him? With each other? Or was it a group of illegals, of whom more than a million entered the United States every year in this sector alone? No, that couldn't be it. They would be anxious to keep moving. They wouldn't stop to make thumping noises.

Mack sneaked a hand over to the radio, but pulled his hand back. He wasn't supposed to break radio silence. He pulled his cell phone from the inside of his fatigue jacket, whipped the clamshell open, and, just as quickly, snapped it shut as a blaze of light nearly blinded him—he'd forgotten it would throw bright blue light all over the place. Now he saw stars. It was like getting a flashbulb in the eyes in the dark, when your pupils were wide open.

As he sat, waiting for bilious green blobs to stop floating before his eyes, he heard a sound like shredding tin.

The noise was loud, and went on for a long minute or two. The echoes bounced around in the shallow river canyon.

He couldn't figure out what it was, but it had to be humans doing something. Or someone not quite human.

Out here, anything was possible. The native people had walked the San Diego River and its tributary streams for thousands of years. They'd migrated seasonally between the mountains to the east, and the beaches to the west. Winter on the beach, where the weather was milder and the fishing good; summers in the mountains, where the hunting was better. They had been in the habit of defleshing their dead and breaking the bones up before putting them in pots and burying them, so that the dead would not walk at night. This was stuff you scoffed at in a downtown San Diego office building by day.

Out here, alone, on the river at night, it wasn't so easy to scoff. In the foothills of the Lagunas, Palomar, Volcan, and other mountains, where wild deer and rattle snakes and mountain lions roamed, it was said the ancient dead sometimes walked on their long-ago trails. Tonight would be such a night, Mack thought as his scalp prickled and cold sweat broke out as his neck tightened. He stopped chewing and listened intently, cradling the gun. He tried to tune in to what was happening out there.

Hearing a cry that could be from a man or woman, strong but high-pitched, he opened the car door and stepped outside.

Holding the gun in his right hand, he cupped his other hand behind his ear and tried not to breathe.

There was no mistaking now—something violent and noisy was happening not far away in the thick, roiling fog in the river basin. Whatever it was, the thick reeds towering twenty feet, and the gloomy oaks and willows, were not giving up their secrets.

He heard a splash and looked down. The quietly flowing river was visible directly below, where the fog was thin. Starlight gleamed on fast-moving water. Something was causing undulating waves.

He heard that cry again, this time of someone in pain. Maybe it was an illegal being mauled by a mountain lion. But there were none of the growls and cat-wails one might expect, not that Mack was an expert in such matters.

Reaching down under the driver's seat, he pulled out his favorite weapon—a three pound, two-foot flashlight of black steel.

He walked into the deepening gloom as far as he could before he had to turn the light on. The fog all around blinded him. He aimed at the ground just ahead of his feet. He walked forward in the glow that must have made him into a target big as an elephant. "Hello?" he called. "Anyone there?"

Silence.

But the thrashing noises continued, and the screech of some strong material being torn, the banging of bending tin or some other metal, continued without respite.

He turned the light off and quickly stepped aside, in case someone or something was targeting him. The light was more of a liability than it was worth.

He stumbled over a large, snaking tree root. In trying to regain his balance, he stepped over the edge of the river bank, landed with one foot on a muddy slope slippery as ice, and slid down until his right boot was in the cold water. The flashlight rolled and bounced, like a carnival wheel, into the water. He caught a last glimpse of it sinking down into feet of soft muck and its glowed dimmed and disappeared. The river here was about thirty feet across, with spots where the muck was like quicksand. He wasn't going after it—too cold, wet, and creepy. The noise would expose him to whatever was going on around a bend in the river.

Getting his sleeves cold and muddy, as well as his rear end and back, he crab-walked backwards up to the road.

A snake rattled loudly and then slithered away into dead bamboo and dry, yellowed reed debris.

He had never dropped his gun. That was in his right hand in an iron grip. Two tours in the Army, with combat in the Middle East and elsewhere, had taught him if you lose everything else, hold on to your weapon and your ammo. You can get another flashlight, another sandwich, another dry shirt or whatever, but you're as good as dead without a means of defense.

He walked around a bend in the road, as it curved with the river, and saw something so strange he shook his head and wiped his hands over his eyes, gun and all.

For a moment, he thought the large metal craft, which hovered some six or eight feet above the water, was a helicopter—but there were no rotors. It was a cross between an egg and a bus, and had three stubby side fins with huge airline-style engines on them.

There was movement in the water below—too much to take in in one glance—people in pilot suits fighting, no helmets—and a dead person hung out of the open hatch.

The dead woman's upper torso lay on the river bank—hair and face burned beyond recognition, skull-teeth glittering. The lower half of her body, from the belt down, still in its flight suit, hung down from a tangle of seatbelt webbing.

The markings on the craft were strange, too—a hodgepodge of cuneiform that looked like chopped salad. He took in all this in a second.

Several men were in the water, punching and beating each other so that the water foamed white all around them.

From the smell of scorched flesh, and acrid smoke in the air, he deduced the woman had been alive minutes earlier. That smoke wasn't gunpowder, though—more like molten metal, or maybe magnesium, tortured with electric currents and extinguished in a mess by dirty water.

The aircraft itself was cream-colored, but dented and blackened around the woman's dangling corpse.

Hearing the radio squawk a few hundred feet away, Mack ran back to the car. At least, being called on the radio was something he could understand. Amazing how far he'd come. He slipped and fell on mud, rolled back upright and kept running. He could hear the voice of Leo Roberts, his partner. "Ten ten, base to Mack, come in, we're scrubbing…"

Before Mack could reach the car, something massive roared along above his head—a black aircraft or space craft studded on all sides with knife-like blades of light.

It wasn't a Federal chopper, but another of these mysterious aircraft with the triple nacelles on stubby wings.

A second later, three or four pillars of light, rippling with grainy purple-green energy popcorn, which sizzled and spluttered, slammed down on the car and melted it down into a mass of smoking, glowing slag.

The heat drove Mack backwards. He tore his cell phone from his inside pocket, whipped the clam open, and with trembling fingers pressed the pre-dials. He held it under his lapel to stanch the blue light, which still leaked out. Leo answered in a tense and gritty voice. "Mack, what's going on?"

"You tell me." As he breathlessly spoke, leaning over the phone, Mack noticed a faintly glowing figure about fifty feet away, a woman, completely encased in a dull gray astronaut garment complete with bubble helmet, intently studying a data tablet held in both hands.

"Mack, speak to me," Leo snapped anxiously.

"Hold on." The screen in the woman's hands sent a faint luminance up against her face plate.

The aircraft above roared away across the desert. Still deafened by the noise, shocked, Mack staggered back a step or two.

He heard a series of popping noises from behind him—men shooting each other in the water.

Dazed, he turned to go back for another look—when a dull, massive pain wrenched his right wrist and made him drop the gun. As he looked at his wrist and went to reach for it with his other hand, a fist crashed into his face. He just glimpsed raw, ochre knuckles and pale, hairy fingers sailing into his face as the lights went out. The cell phone fell to the ground and was lost.

He awoke minutes later, lying on his back on soft damp soil, with pain around his right eye, as if the blow had splintered the bony edges of the orbit. His nose had been mashed painfully, and someone had laid a thick, absorbent cloth smelling of disinfectant over his face.

He sputtered and sat up. He held the cloth to his wet nose and uttered a groan of protest. Holding his fingers up, he saw dark liquid on the tips—his nose blood.

"Don't get any ideas," said a powerful looking man with short dark hair, wearing a flight suit but no helmet. "Don't try to get up or I may have to shoot you."

Mack detected an indefinable accent. He heard two or three persons arguing, one of them female. From the frantic tone, he guessed they wouldn't have time for niceties, and might just save time by plugging him with a quick bullet or two—or whatever flew out of those complex, spidery black weapons two of them carried with an upraised arm.

He rolled over onto his side and dabbed his nose. He caught a glimpse of the hovering craft. Several bodies had been dragged onto the river bank, each with large dark spots that smelled like charred flesh and might be partly blood. The half-torso still hung out of the wrecked craft.

"We kill him—here—now." The man's voice radiated at Mack from behind, as if he were looking at Mack while saying it.

"I have data on him. We need him," said a female voice. He looked over his shoulder. The woman dangled her helmet in one hand and the data tablet in the other.

"We have to take him with us," said a second man. "Naria is right."

They put their heads together and mumbled excitedly. At one point, Mack thought he heard one say Carly. Couldn't be. His dear, sweet wife, a public school nurse—what could she possibly have to do with this nightmare? He must have heard wrong. He felt a surge of adrenalin, a desperate urgency to get home to his wife.

He tossed the towel aside, sprang to his feet, and sprinted down the road.

He was going uphill at a slight grade, and left the fog behind.

As he rose above the little river valley, and the reedy swamps on each sides in the meanders, he came into a clearing.

The desert road was bright enough to see small boulders, as well as big ruts, so he was able to maintain a good running clip.

A bright light sprang up behind him, illumining the area.

He veered off the road and continued running in light trees and balls of scrub. He had been a jogger most of his life. He had good wind, and went into long-distance mode.

The ground rose and fell, and he kept up the pace. His breath sawed raggedly, and his boots pounded the ground.

The light behind him faded.

The air was cool and clear, with stars twinkling rapidly in a fast-moving Santa Ana wind high up. He hadn't caught anything on the weather news about a Santa Ana Condition, but he'd grown up in San Diego, and knew the signs. The air had an aching, disturbed sense. It was downright chilly at night. Days were sunny and hot, with bone-dry air whipping around in strong winds. He thought of Carly, and wished he could call her to warn her to lock the doors, but he'd lost his phone. He hoped she was okay. He could picture her smiling with rouged lips as she made his tuna sandwich. And he'd lost the sandwich, dammit! He wasn't hungry anymore, but he loved that sandwich because she had made it, and he loved her, and felt saddened by its loss in the inferno of the car.

What am I thinking?

He felt light-headed. His jacket was open, and his shirt was wet. He touched his nose and felt wetness—he saw dark liquid on his fingers. His nose was bleeding again. By all rights, he should stop and lie down. That was it. Lie on your back with your head tilted back. He didn't have time for that now. He had to get away from these people, whoever they were. Maybe Leo and the boss were somewhere nearby. They could call in the Border Patrol, the Navy, the Marines, the Sheriff, Tribal Police from the reservations…there was enough fire power in the area. Could he get away far enough and long enough to join up with some of them? That was the question.

Have to try. Have to try. Have to try.

He made it a mantra, reciting it silently in his head as he lifted one foot, then the other.

Down, up, left, right, down, up, left, right…

He was a machine, pumping through the dry, cold air that smelled of creosote and lavender, mesquite, all the subtle hardy aromas baked all day. Even the sand and the stone here had a warm, almost nutty smell like the inside of an oven. It was, after all, Anza-Borrego, one of the hottest deserts on earth. With that jumble of thoughts crashing around in the dryer of his thoughts, he tripped over a small agave plant and went sailing, head first, head over heels, into a small canyon.

His head luckily only rolled on sand, and he brushed innocuously against boulders that could have been fatal if he'd hit them with his head. He was in a cleft about 30 feet deep. From the shape of it, it looked like a pair of ancient sand dunes sculpted within the thirty to ninety foot-deep bays of a primordial ocean that had covered most of the U.S. Southwest. Giant sharks the size of moving vans had once swum here, devouring prey the size of a pickup truck.

Mack rose to his feet in the silence and darkness, and started charging up the other side. He was going at a good clip. He glanced back and saw only darkness. He heard nothing. This was good. He started running hard as soon as he hit the flat land above.

A ship size of a city block rose up from behind.

Its underside was steely and gleamed with a faint golden light.

It was covered with lights, windows, bays, doors, ladders, coils of cable rolled up and fastened for travel.

It had a head the size and shape of one of those long ago sharks.

The nose of the vehicle was black and had bluish-white running lights that shone ahead like headlights.

He was framed in a mess of fine, darting beams of light.

The ship made a sighing, hissing sound, like someone breathing. It gurgled faintly, like someone breathing underwater. Its engines had a deep, shuddering quality, almost silent, but Mack could feel the power in them. He fell and rolled over onto his back. He put his hands up defensively as the bright lights closed in on him. He felt the ship's throbbing in the ground all around him. He remembered a description an old-timer had once given in a TV interview in black and white, of seeing the Zeppelin Hindenburg fly overhead in the 1930s. Her engines made this slow, throbbing sound:

wobb… wobb… wobb… wobb…

He glimpsed eight or ten nacelles making a similar pulsing noise. As the ship descended over him like a manta ray, a twin hatch opened up and darkness closed over him.

He curled into a ball and yelled a defiant curse as the doorway descended over him like a giant mouth.

The ship's lights were like eyes, its nose like a shark's. They had him.

He smelled something that must be an anaesthetic gas, a faintly nauseous mix of lime and melon aromas—and he went blank.

City at the
End of Time

2. Time Trains Uptime—Membrane Medicine

Mack hovered in and out of a coma as the woman named Naria came and went from the small, antiseptic cell where they kept him—whoever 'they' were.

He kept dreaming of Carly and their kitchen back home. She was fixing him a tuna sandwich on toast, with the edges trimmed off. She poured them each a glass of Zinfandel and handed him his glass with a sweet smile. Her dark red lipstick opened into a smile as her eyes twinkled and her delicate shoulders shrugged coyly. He reached out for her, but the wine glass fell and shattered on the floor. Carly kept smiling and did not seem to notice. Her lips moved but he could not hear what she was saying. Shadows with knives and baseball bats moved on the wall behind her.

What's happening to me?

My name is Naria, said a woman's assured, cool voice. *I am a doctor. We have to prep you for the Temporale. It's a law of the Time Train universe.*

He heaved, curling up violently several times in rapid succession.

You will be better soon, I promise. We don't do the surgery. The Membrane, the border into the Temporale, does this. We've all been through it, Mr. Mackinson. It doesn't hurt afterwards. You'll see. Then you can travel among the worlds without worry about viruses and anomalies. The Membrane will now take over.

What about Carly, dammit?

He thrashed about, vomiting, unable to talk. She was a white-coated, dark-haired authority, a woman, a cold nurturer, hovering by his gurney amid all the steel and glass and porcelain in this tiny cabin. If the shark-ship's eight nacelles were pounding away, somewhen out in time, somewhere amid the tumbling galaxies like water pouring from a spigot, he could not feel the faintest tremor of their powerful pulses. Oh yes, if he listened carefully, there it was:

wobb... wobb... wobb... wobb...

I am sorry for all that we have to put you through. And I am sorry about Carla.

What? What do you mean sorry about Carla?

The only good news I can offer is that you will see the City of the Universe shortly. You will never be the same again, Mr. Mackinson.

There Carly was again, in the kitchen, but this time there was no wine. There was no tuna fish salad sandwich. Her hands were folded on the counter where she stood, wearing her dark blue summer dress with the green and orange flower petals on it. Her shoulders were bare, and her straight hair dangled in a page boy. Her expression was rueful, her mouth a sad, dark-red oval, her eyes a somber blue.

No!

Mack tried to thrash as the surgical team came out of the walls, but he was pinioned and helpless. Nobody spoke now. The chief surgeon—they were all tied to the wall by threads and tubes, so they had to be androids—was a tall, thin femalish expert whose skin glistened like black and white checkered milk-glass, with gold thread dividing the tiles. Her face was lovely but frozen like alabaster. Her eyes were long and narrow and angled.

Welcome to surgery, sweetheart.

Her lips were silver, and almost smiling. She radiated a cool kindness that was mostly about helping herself get the job done by reassuring the patient. Her fine fingers were ebony, and moved with machine precision. Her assistants were ivory angels who held lancets and spritzers and trumpets and bandages while they sang in a Gregorian chorus, but no prayer known on earth. The chief surgeon did not speak, but she emoted.

We'll get you all fixed up, Mack.

He was paralyzed, but tried to squint in the twisted light that filled the room like warm honey full of busily working bees.

Carly?

It's all in your mind, darling. Hold still while I insert the bramlets and inck your morells. Your skin will become impervious to things like the common cold. You won't devastate entire alien populations with the flu bug. You'll live for thousands of years.

I want my wife. I want a glass of wine and a tuna fish sandwich in my kitchen.

You can have a glass of Zinfandel and a tuna fish sandwich when you get to the City of En. Time Town. City of the Universe. Hold still.

Carly…

He tried to reach out toward his wife in the kitchen.

Oh yes, that.

The surgeon yanked on something that came loose.

That's better.

Mack saw an empty house with no furniture, no wife—nothing but a faint sunbeam streaking in to land on the dusty wooden floor. He felt a wrenching sense of loss. He emitted a long telepathic sob that tore from him like the nerve junctures she was removing and replacing with gold alloys fine as spider weavings. The sense of loss faded as he walked from his house of memory and the door clicked gently shut behind him, forever.

The surgeon's busy black hands glittered wetly. Her fingers wriggled skillfully like spider legs in the smoky, icy blue surgical light above their heads.

He was here in the forever.

Almost done. You are becoming amortal, Mack. Without death. Your nervous system is turning to glassy fibers. Only your brain won't change. You can live almost forever, unless a truck hits you…

He saw a blurry image of a road in a lovely green field, and a big rig bearing down on him with blaring air horns.

…or you fall into a star…

He saw an image of a great ship with a thousand nacelles, smoking and on fire, its nose starting to glow, and ten thousand passengers screaming telepathically, as its glowing heat shield dipped into the melt-field of an orange star the color of liquid lava.

…or an hourglass-weaver-spider comes out of its nest and stings you with mortality if you're not careful…

He was on a glassy moon that had been blasted by meteors for eons, and a spider-like thing with an hourglass-shaped head scuttled out from under a boulder. Desperately, he clambered up a wire ladder to enter back into the derelict ship that had brought him here on a silent cruise.

Like a symphony, the surgery was coming to a climax.

Snip went thread.

Black hands glowed in a wet blur.

Clang, went scissors into a surgical tray. It was all metaphor, of course. Somehow, he knew that, even though he was whacked out on some hallucinomeds. The Membrane morphed into a surgical station and altered him so he could move through the interstices of time and space as a fish darts through water.

The angels held scalpels and offered towels and cups of anaesthetic while singing in high, chirping voices.

Their faces were feminine but indistinct, their heads like those of veiled nuns.

A thousand old men with white hair leaned over their cellos and dragged bows across strings.

In unison, they made a long golden sound that needed no pause for breath, that dragged on for hours in a perfect chord...

* * * *

A man and a woman, each wearing gloves and safety glasses, led him by the elbows down a long corridor. Mack shuffled along in his refurbished body. The people guiding him wore white coats that blended with the too-bright lighting and the snowy walls. He slept for a long time and had no dreams.

A public address system crackled briefly and then a woman's sensuous, laughing voice flowed out like honey, echoing among the frigid walls:" Welcome to the Temporale. Thank you for choosing TRANSENT, the Transportation Entity of the City of the Universe. Welcome aboard, and have a pleasant trip to your connecting destination. Enjoy your journey across space and time as we make sure you arrive safely and punctually."

Mack felt enraged and grieving, without knowing why. His entire body tingled numbly with hidden pain. He wrenched himself free by turning his body left and right and flailing his heavy arms. He couldn't quite lift his arms, so he threw his weight at the man at his left elbow. The man grabbed him in a bear hug. As Mack's head rolled back over his shoulder, he saw the woman raising a hypodermic gun while her glasses glittered coldly. There was no needle as she pressed the gun to his forehead—just a puff of air smelling faintly like cloves.

He faded...

3. Time Town

When Mack awoke, he was comfortably strapped into a plush chair in a semi-dark room. His hands were loosely clasped in his lap, over a thin blanket covering his lower torso and upper legs. A seatbelt secured him to the high backed chair. He wore a brown jumpsuit and soft, comfortable black slippers. He was sitting a bit laid back, with his legs crossed at the ankles.

A gray cat with golden eyes purred and rubbed against his slippers. The cat looked at him questioningly.

"Cats are always about lunch," Mack said to the cat. Mack looked around at the richly carpeted floor, the books on the walls, a ladder to reach the high shelves, a small wooden coffee table whose top was finished with red Morocco leather. It reminded him of being on a train, in an odd way, because there was an empty seat beside him, and two empty seats faced him. He strained to look over his shoulder, and saw more facing arrangements fading into darkness behind him. On his right was a great big circle made of brass, like the rim of a clock, a shining band about six inches wide. Unlike a clock, there was nothing but blank wall on the surface inside the circle.

The cat squeezed its eyes shut and opened them, a gesture of greeting. It yawned, showing razor teeth and a pink tongue. It emitted a yowl of need.

"I wish I had something to give you. But I don't know where we are, or what's going on. I don't know why, and I hardly remember who I am."

The door opened, and several young men and women poured in. They wore dark blue smocks, dark trousers, and soft boots. They brought a tray of food, a tray of medicine, a data tablet, all sorts of other junk and equipment. With them were an older man and woman, both 60ish and dressed elegantly in black. Their clothing looked almost like normal 21st Century business attire. As two pretty young technicians swung open a shelf in the armrest, on which to put his breakfast, the older woman rubbed her hands together briskly and sat in the seat opposite Mack, next to the wall. "Well, well, Mr. Mackinson, it looks like we have you put to rights. Are you comfortable?"

The oldish man petted the cat and picked it up. "I see you have met Donald."

Mack shrugged. "I have no idea where I am or what's going on. I remember being in pain, but not any more. I can't remember..."

The older man let the cat go, which ran away. The man joined her in the other facing seat. "Of course, Mack. You don't remember much of anything, and you won't remember us when we're done. Go on, eat your breakfast. I hope it's to your liking."

As the technicians started to leave, Mack lifted a metal lid on his tray. He saw under it two eggs on a plate, sunny side up; several strips of bacon cooked just to the edge of crisp, the way he liked it, the way...[someone]...used to make it; an English muffin with butter melting in its just-browned peaks; and black coffee. "No orange juice?" A technician anxiously ran from the room. The older man said: "We're getting it for you as we speak." He handed Mack a card made of a white plastic-like material—a digital business card. Mack saw their images on it—and salad-mix alphabet writing. The calligraphy had a certain busy though orderly elegance—almost Chinese—but still reminded Mack of an explosion in a noodle factory. "You may call me Tenc, and this is The Honorable Lady Chivet Betize, Third Postal Lord. I am General Tenc Hoseth of the Postal Service." The way he said it, her last name sounded like 'beat haze.' The calligraphy floated, sort of turned in its watery digital grave, and sensible American English letters drifted up into view, so he knew how to spell these foreign names.

Mack chortled. He put the card aside. Postal Lord? "Let me taste this to see if it's real." He picked up a bacon slice and chewed on it. Made his mouth water. "It's good! I seem to remember being a policeman in the United States, but it's all very dim." He shifted positions, eager to stand, but didn't quite have the strength in his legs. He did manage to undo the seatbelt. Seatbelt? In a library?

"What's your last memory?" asked Lady Betize. She looked a healthy, tan sixty with smooth skin just beginning to wrinkle. Her hair was silvery and full, combed in a wave with a gold comb in it. General Hoseth looked like a puffy haw haw in those tea commercials, one eye slightly larger than the other. His wrinkles were more pronounced than hers. His hair was long and combed over one side, a bit mussy.

Mack thought hard as he stared at the two. A young blonde woman in a smock rushed to his side with a glass of chilled orange juice. "I see me standing at the edge of a river. It's foggy. There is a craft of some kind hovering there. A UFO. There's a dead body hanging out the door, and there are people fighting in the water."

"That's it?" asked Lady Betize. She looked at Hoseth, and they both nodded in satisfaction.

"There's more," Mack said, struggling to push further in time.

They instantly looked at him with worry.

"Something about a car…blowing up…fire from the sky…a huge UFO overhead…"

"Go on," Hoseth urged, as if offering poisoned meat to a strange dog. Mack got the reading: these people were not his friends. But were they his enemies? There was something warlike and ruthless about them.

Mack shook his head. A kitchen. Pain. He shook his head, trying to free the memory.

"Your orange juice," said LadyBetize. She and Haw Haw both eyeballed the glass the girl had just brought.

"Are you going to kill me?"

Her face widened in shock, and he guffawed. "Kill you! Haw haw! That's rich. We just saved your life." He laughed until he turned red, slapping his knees with his hands, until she jabbed him in the side with her elbow. She took over, saying: "Mr. Mackinson, we need your help. It's not a matter of choice for either you, or us."

He picked up the orange juice and sipped a little. It was just perfect—cool, tart, orangey. He drank it down thirstily, closing his eyes, and that vision of a kitchen morphed into someone else's house. The other people's kitchen table had a brass vase on it with red, white, and blue flowers, on a white crocheted doily. There were some letters and a small package on the corner of the table, waiting to be opened when the strangers who lived here came home from work. A strange dog barked at Mack—a little black and white Boston terrier. Mack apologized to the jumping, anxious dog. Mack let himself out, promising never to intrude again, and turned the lock so that, when he clicked the door shut, nobody including himself could enter without a key.

Lady Betize glowed. "That's more like it."

General Hoseth leaned forward. "Mr. Mackinson, you won't remember this meeting when you go into the field. We do have to explain a few things to you, so that certain instructions will remain in your deep memory where neither you, nor our enemies, nor our allies, nor the Long War government of your people will be able to read them. Your mission will be very important to our nation, and we thank you ahead of time for your commitment."

"Why should I do anything for you?"

"Bravo," Hoseth said, "now we're down to the nub of it."

"There's the key, isn't it?" said Lady Betize.

Mack got it. He didn't know what they were holding over him, but it was something so colossal and soul-smashing that he knew he had no choice but to comply with their wishes.

"Sadly, Mr. Mackinson, our government is forced to not always play gently. In a few moments you'll see why. We have our backs against the wall. We're fighting for our lives, and the little things that you people have done in the past grow and grow, the way a sound will go out, and sympathetic tuning forks pick up on it, and soon a whole world is humming with that sound. Waves of do and don't propagate like light, Mr. Mackinson."

"What on earth are you talking about?"

"On earth," Hoseth said with a nod.

"In the future," Lady Betize. "Look." She lifted a finger to the wall beside her. A button appeared out of nowhere, and she pressed it. Inside the great brass framing circle, the wall turned into a giant viewing screen. Mack jumped back. For an instant he felt a shock of vertigo as trillions of miles of outer space hung frozen on his right.

"Don't worry," she said. "It's a solid wall. What you are seeing is a tubed image captured on the outside and broadcast on this viewing screen. It's just like having a window, but without all the silly glass that would be so fragile."

"What is this?" Mack said.

"Eat your breakfast and you'll find out."

"Huh?" He stared at the two wiggly eggs with their happy yellow eyes, and the bacon which he'd been nibbling.

"Meme cocktails," said Haw Haw. "It would take us years to explain it all. Eat and you'll understand."

"Before it gets cold," she added in a motherly fashion.

Hoseth added: "We have to pour it all into you. Time is something we don't have enough of here, even though it's Time Town. You'll see why. We are literally running out of time."

Mack ate his breakfast. Servers brought him more coffee, and tea for his hosts. As he ate, he looked out and started to get it. The coffee particularly seemed to jolt those tiny memory clusters into his bloodstream, whence they rushed into his brain and joined their fellow bioelectrical constructs dancing around on the wetly glistening folds of the cortices. As he drank his coffee, it all became clear to Mack. His era was critical in the history of mankind, because (broadly) his contemporaries discovered the true cosmos beyond the Milky Way, and made the first fledgling steps in to space. The cosmos, the Temporale, and Time Town explained themselves to him, direct from his breakfast to the brain.

The onslaught of data was overwhelming. Information poured into his paralyzed body and wide-alert brain as the cosmic repair shop of the far future prepped him for a mission he was about to undertake in 2049 CE.

Cosmic Secrets

4. Meme Juice, Part I: the Cosmos (Exogravitation)

Author's Note: Light Readers, You May Skip This Chapter.

In the 1920s, a young astronomer named Edwin Hubble, using the 100 inch Hooker Telescope, announced that the Milky Way was not the entire universe. It was one of several major discoveries of his generation that would change history. A short while earlier, a Swiss patent office clerk had published his Theory of Relativity, which made the Newtonian universe obsolete as a complete explanation of the universe. Hubble also demonstrated that the incredibly vast universe, in which the Milky Way galaxy was barely a pinprick, was expanding.

By the close of the century, cosmology—the study of the universe—was once again in disarray because of three great enigmas. Science was shocked to discover that not only was the universe expanding, but the rate of expansion was increasing. It was speeding up. How could that be? It seemed a violation of basic laws of science. Had the extra energy (so-called dark energy) required to accelerate the expansion been hidden somewhere all along? Or was it coming from outside?

Astronomers had not yet officially begun to speak of 'outside.' That would imply, as the Milky Way is but a molecule in vast cosmic ocean of galaxies, our very universe is a molecule in an infinite and eternal ocean of universes.

Beyond 'dark energy' and the accelerating expansion was a third mystery—dark matter. By the end of Hubble's century, scientists had discovered that the mass of the universe was only a few per cent visible. Most of the universe consisted of a previously unknown substance that was unseen and unknowable, which gained the nickname called 'dark matter'.

As science reeled in disarray at these enigmas, the solution was revealed to be astoundingly simple. The force causing the expansion of the universe to constantly accelerate was none other than gravity, and this gravity was coming from outside the universe. That—the existence of a larger structure, the realization that our universe is not the whole thing but only a tiny part of it— caused the next revolution in cosmology. It was the understanding, finally, that there exists an infinite and eternal motherverse containing endless universes that are born, live, and die in an endless cycle.

The existence of a larger structure has immediate implications. Since its gravity is pulling our universe apart, and since the dead cinders of our universe will spill out there, the motherverse must contain something that generates gravity. That something is a neither a particle of matter nor energy, but a platelet of pure gravity—the godot. The godot is the irreducible bottom floor of elementary substances. It is so tiny that, if it were a grain of sand, a hydrogen atom next to it would seem as large as the solar system.

Our universe is being pulled apart by the ambient gravity of the motherverse. As the universe expands, pushing its edge (the cosmopause) ever farther and more rapidly outward, the universe decays back to elemental gravity platelets. In the motherverse, there are no light or matter—just infinitely many such platelets (a bit like the black stones in a game of Go, hence 'godots') drifting around in a random Brownian motion. Their drifting is the kinetic energy mentioned. If there is any visible energy, it is the distant glow from stars and galaxies inside universes. As the godots drift in the motherverse, they gradually gather into clumps. Drifting clumps join other clumps, slowly gathering into a larger and larger gravity locus. A clump of godots grows, slowly at first, then faster and faster, becoming an accretion sphere. Faster and faster, the accretion sphere vacuums more platelets or godots to itself, until it reaches Critical Mass 1 or C-1.

At that point, the overwhelming gravity (still its only property, except all that kinetic energy has become potential energy, a vast amount at C-1) causes the sphere to implode.

At the low point of this inflection, C-2, the pent up energy is so vast that the sphere goes Bang, as in Big Bang. Only it does not quite just explode, based on the evidence of what comes next.

It fragments like a grenade (C-3), throwing out three kinds of debris that can be detected.

The first kind of C-3 (Free) debris are enormous quantities of free godots or platelets that make up 80% of the universe and are the so-called dark matter, except there is no matter there, just raw gravity, which, in a dark room, seems just like mass. These could poetically be called star dust.

The second kind of C-3 (Heavy) debris are fragments of the accretion sphere that have not yet come apart. They become free-flying, spinning black holes of violent energy and enormous gravity.

The third, and rarest, kind of C-3 (Visible) debris is visible matter. Constituting about 4% of the whole, this is matter whose godot platelets are more loosely stuck together than in the black holes, but they are far more adhesive than the free godots. One could say that, in the Heavy, godots are jammed together, while in the Visible the platelets merely stick to each other.

Seventy-five percent of intermediate visible matter is hydrogen, 24% is helium, and the remaining 1% is everything else, including people, cats, dogs, planets, and stars. Most is captured around C-3-Heavy black holes, much of it energetic and luminous, giving normal galaxies a characteristic shape as multi-armed, whirling pancakes of luminosity. Only a tiny part of a galaxy is thus visible. Looming around the visible stars is a much greater cloud of C-3 Dark, and at the core of the galaxy a great attractor, the C-3 Heavy black hole.

At the bottom floor of 'stuff,' far below baryons and mesons, the terminally small unit is the godot, and both C-3-Heavy and C-3-Visible are ultimately composed of pure gravity (godots) platelets jammed together. The universe has a transient lifetime that must eventually end (thirty billion years out, perhaps) as the pent up energy from C-1, C-2, and C-3 dissipates. Matter sticks around for a while, but not forever. The great destructor is the ambient gravity of the motherverse, the most powerful force in nature. Within a universe, visible matter itself has gravity and tends to lump together. Beyond 80 Jupiters in size, it starts to become a full-fledged star. Between 20 and 80 Jupiters, it forms a brown dwarf. There are smaller and larger animals in the menagerie, including the heavy elements that form earthlike planets, while others form large, violent stars like novae and supernovae.

The initial C-3 fragmentation gives a push that slows geometrically because of the aggregate gravitation of the local universe. But the ambient gravity of the motherverse is the most powerful force in nature; it accelerates the process of pulling the universe apart in all directions. (The problem of colliding or even proximate universes is another matter not covered in Mack's meme soup this day). As the cosmopause rushes ever faster outward in all directions, the architecture of the universe starts to attenuate. Structures fall apart, and the pieces evaporate. Technically, this ultimately becomes about the same thing as entropy. First, the visible stuff disappears. The free godots roam about as star dust. Gradually, what's left of the black holes drifts away and becomes seed material for new universes out in the motherverse. Some of the dark matter platelets of pure gravity thrown out by C-3 can rejoin those black holes in making a new universe.

This is the whole enchilada. It's an eternal cycle that forms and destroys infinitely many universes in infinitely many places in eternal amounts of time. It's the motherverse.

Mack was about one third done with his breakfast. He continued eating with relish, and could almost feel those powerful memes and tiny Rules popping out of their packages and populating his brain with more information. Now that he understood the universe and the motherverse, he could understand the Temporale.

5. Meme Juice, Part II: Temporale

Author's Note: Light Readers, You May Skip This Chapter.

More than a billion years ago, inside our universe, a forgotten super-race of beings constructed a self-replicating mechanism called the Temporale. It is a transportation system that cuts across the natural limits of time and space. It successfully creates a way of going sideways around natural laws limiting the speed of travel, approaching an absolute ceiling near the speed of light.

Though we have no writing or other contact left from these long-ago aliens, we think they approached their project as a neural engineering problem, using what are called Rules. Rules use the tendency of successful evolutionary constructs (like human DNA, or the star-building process) to repeat themselves.

Repetition is the fundamental requirement for a successfully evolved construct. Everything, whether it is the making of a star from the simple accretion of hydrogen and helium, to the accretion of universes in the motherverse, to the reproduction of humans and other creatures on earth, is driven by gravity and functions through processes that automatically repeat themselves. The basic process is entirely dumb and brute force, but complexity sets in quickly and exponentially. Just as intelligent life evolves (and intelligence is relative in some regards, based on function and need, but absolute in the sense that its function approaches a limit based on neurological factors such as synaptic speed, connective limitations, and the like) so the Temporale has evolved a necessary level of intelligence. That intelligence is known as the Membrane, because one of the naturally evolved functions of the Temporale is the need to stop the spread of destructive viruses, be they in the network of the Temporale itself, or in beings that travel in the Temporale. Mack's advanced surgery had just been performed by Rules, expressed in metaphors, but literally enacted in a physical operating theater manned by temporary gestalts created by the Membrane.

The Temporale hooks up points inside the universe by using roadways outside, in the motherverse.

The Membrane is an invisible shield around the long roadways of the Temporale, and its inwarded cities and domed lands. The Membrane is also inherent in the material of the Temporale itself.

If a part of the Temporale is injured, say by a black hole doing a few excess energy burps as it digests its accompanying galaxy of visible matter, then the Temporale reaches down into the fundamental subfloor of the motherverse for the necessary godots to rebuild itself through replication and Rules. The Temporale can also use fundamental particle-energy physics in a sort of alchemy developed by the ancients to transmute many substances into others as needed, and there is usually enough solar or hydrogen/helium power available to drive the process.

The aliens are long gone, but their mysterious roadways through time and space serve many later cultures. Over a billion years, the Temporale has grown until one can travel and jump vast amounts of space. Empires have come and gone, wrapped around these pathways, the way rivers and roadways once connected earthly empires like Egypt and Mesopotamia.

As Mack started scarfing down the last third of his breakfast, he was coming to the most fascinating part of this new world. Deep down, something very faint and disturbing gnawed at the very bones of his soul, but neither he nor his hosts were conscious that at least one little tiny Carly meme had survived.

6. Meme Juice, Part III: City of the Universe

Though the star field outside Mack's window seemed static, the train was in fact moving very fast, outside time and space in the Motherverse. Within that great, shiny brass circle that looked like the frame around a clock face, a city in space was now visible. Slowly, a vast array of lights came into view: The City of the Universe (COTU), also known as Time Town; or as the greatest number of all numbers (infinity) impossible to actually reach, N— The City of En, or COEN, in the complex bureaucratic pontifications of its many administrative branches. Its history and structure and meaning were very complex. But its dire situation was easy to understand, and brutally simple: the city was dying. Long ago, a time war had fractured the cosmopause, causing it to disintegrate in this sector.

Mack saw that the city's clouds of light had structures embedded. The lights emanated from those structures—buildings, blocks, entire cities, continents, he could not yet determine. The City of En consisted of innumerable blocks of these lights and structures, like a wall of carefully dressed stones put together without mortar. Each piece was discrete, but they interlocked as an entirety. The city stretched in all directions as far as he could see, as the train drifted into the city. The structures resolved into city blocks, most of them elongated cubes about a thousand feet squared at the end sides, and three times as long on the longer faces. It was as if you took all the neon-drenched cities of Mack's future, all the New Yorks and Tokyos and Londons and Parises and more, and stacked them on top of each other. You could traverse in all perpendicular directions among the cubic city blocks.

In the open spaces among the blocks, traffic flowed—space borne buses, trucks, cars, even one-person hooded motorcycles, for lack of better terms, though all seemed to have some form of that nacelle or jet engine. Many of the vehicles were quite stylish.

Mack gasped. "How big is this city?"

Hoseth said: "It's immeasurable, literally. This was once earth as you know it. Or knew it. The original Temporale port grew and grew until earth became just one part of an agglomeration of objects orbiting the sun. Now the sun itself is buried deep down in the Junkall, and the complex forms a kind of huge wheel orbiting the sun. We moved the three other terrane planets into safe orbits and they are now covered with glowing cities and green forests."

"Is there air out there?" Mack asked.

"Some parts are breathable. Most aren't. You still need a vacuum suit in many areas, and all these vehicles you see are essentially traveling in open space. Many of the city blocks are enclosed in a transparent sort of horn-glass, borne of the Temporale Membrane. In the centers of the city, most of the blocks are linked by breathable horn-glass tunnels."

"Overwhelming," Mack said. Lights from passing vehicles flowed over their faces in a gentle tissue of colors. The flowing colors were almost a song, a hymn, a solemn celebration of such glory. "And you say this place is in trouble?"

Hoseth pointed far out in the distance, where auroras of light shimmered in a grayish mist. "Look carefully, and you'll see parts of the city disintegrating. That's the cosmopause over there. Locals refer to it as the Dissolve. Each solar year, it gets a bit thinner. We're at the edge of space-time, flying apart with the universe. We wouldn't be there at all, if it weren't for a great time war ages ago."

"What's beyond there?" Mack asked, though he knew. The memes were still unpacking on his cortices.

"Nothing," Hoseth said. "Extinction. Death."

She said: "The factions of an extinct empire used inconceivable bombs on each other. Time bombs."

Hoseth said: "In the centuries after your time, our race progressed to space travel and discovered a node of the Temporale near the moon. Ships traveled through it, around it, past it, for generations, before someone realized there was an invisible portal into the motherverse and the Temporale. Our race developed into one of the great star faring people of the Temporale. Nobody knows or owns all of it. We've encountered alien races in far-flung places. We developed a vast trading empire that still exists."

She added: "We reached our limit thousands of years ago. Our job now is a defensive position, to hold what we have, to keep outsiders back. That's half our job. The other half is to tinker with the past. Yes, it can be done. The changes must not be big ones, or they cause a branch universe to pop out, and that does them good, but nothing for us. It's the tiny, very carefully engineered little changes that give us the most hope. If we do them wrong, the future changes, and the cosmopause shrinks a bit relative to the city, and more blocks break off and vanish into godots. If we do the right thing, then we gain an hour, a year, a decade if we're lucky."

"What you would call tweaks," Hoseth said.

Mack asked: "Do you ever get back what you lost?"

She shook her head ruefully. "No, I'm afraid not. Once a city block is gone, it's gone for good. But if we manage to do a good tweak, then of course the past changes and therefore the future, and a whole different bunch of blocks may be there. We don't always know it, either. It's very complex to monitor small changes in the city that are due to our tinkering."

Hoseth cut in: "We are actually at war with each other, quite seriously. That brings me to the final point. There are three major policies at work, although there are many factions that sometimes work together or against each other in complicated ways."

"Usually it's a balance,' she said. "At other times, our people murder each other like in the Cold War not long before your time. The constitutional empire, which is run by several directors and two consuls, with a figurehead emperor, wants us to do nothing. They feel there is too much danger in tinkering. Just move people out when another block is about to sizzle away into godots."

Hoseth said: 'Remember I said we rescued you from TRANSENT?"

Mack nodded. He remembered the woman's voice on the public address system—welcome to our ship and all that happy airline sort of stuff.

"TRANSENT is more radical than our organization. Transportation Entity runs roads and railroads, particularly in the Temporale, which means throughout the city also. We run the Postal Entity. We're POSENT. Our philosophy is to make minimal tinkers. Because we have cargo rights on all moving stock, we are everywhere that TRANSENT goes. Often, our agents work together. Sometimes…"

Mack interrupted: "What do you mean, agents?"

He said: "You have your different government agencies, I'm sure, and they have their own police and intelligence units.'

She scoffed. "If they don't, they should." There was a lot in her veiled look that she wasn't saying.

Hoseth said darkly: "Well, you can use your imagination, Mr. Mackinson…"

"Oh, I see," Mack said. "You're in our time, manipulating."

"Tinkering," she corrected. "Tiny little tweaks, only."

"Right," Hoseth said. "Say that our CloudMaster reasoning machines in the imperial information centers have done a calculation. Let's say they figure that a certain civil servant back in a critical age, say 1943, will accidentally run over a child going to school, and this child happens to be the little son of a major atomic scientist. The atomic scientist receives a call, and rushes to the hospital where his child critically ill. He stays there for days on end, missing some critical brainstorming sessions with Dr. Oppenheimer and General Groves, let's say, and thus a discovery he could have announced that day will be delayed for weeks. TRANSENT would send someone back to shoot the man in the car. POSENT would send someone back to yank the child back onto the sidewalk as the car goes by. The imperial bureaucracy, or Taxing Entity, also known as TAXENT, would do nothing and hope for the best. TAXENT also has an intelligence arm called EXENT, Executive Entity, which they might send into the field to interfere with both TRANSENT and POSENT agents. The TRANSENT person might kill both the driver and the POSENT agent, and on and on it goes…so you see it's a very dangerous and complex game with many possible combinations."

"On top of it, we have external enemies—some are aliens, some are more or less humanoid, humansh, humanish, what have you—there are countless national entities outside our own that have a stake in this, too. Some want us gone so they can grab our enormous trade empire. Others depend on our wealth and protection, though most would stab us in the back if it were the more appealing option."

"Confusing, even with all these memes in my system," Mack said.

"I know," Hoseth said grimly. "And now, Mr. Mackinson, with no time to waste, we must add to your information store."

"What was TRANSENT going to do with me?'

Hoseth deliberated. "I can't say, Mr. Mackinson. I can tell you it would be something far more drastic than we plan."

She rose and took a capsule from a plastic-like baggie in her pocket. She handed the capsule to Mack, who sat back and eyeballed the thing dubiously. She jerked her wrist insistently. "Take it, Mr. Mackinson. Remember our subliminal conversation a little while ago. Whizzago." She snapped her fingers, turning on the hypnosis they had just secretly engineered in him.

"Whizzago," he repeated dully. He was under hypnotic control, and he couldn't fight them. The activator was this nonsense word, which sort of vaguely rhymed with San Diego. It was the trigger to remind him of something, a fear, a loss, a terror, buried so deeply in his soul that he couldn't remember it, but knew he would give his life. He accepted the capsule, and swallowed it with the last of his coffee.

Hoseth started to explain the mission. "You will not remember this meeting, Mr. Mackinson. You will temporarily forget even the things you learned about cosmology, the Temporale, and Time Town. That capsule will suppress your knowledge long enough to get done what you need to do. You'll also have a temporary identity that will shield you from government scans."

"Let's get to it then," said Lady Betize. Golden blocks moved slowly past as they spoke. The library car had a cozy gloom to it, while stained glass color panes moved over the features of those in the room. Traffic flowed by in an ever thickening stream, revealing the energy and wealth of a city that was at the same time in danger of crumbling into nothing.

"You're going back to the late 21st Century, Mr. Mackinson, in the Year 2049. You will need to be cautious. Watch your step, and look for agents from the future if there are any. Some would be there to harm you, others to help you…"

Track 04. The Great Shepherd

Terror is Healthy

7. Kenny C. Del Sol

The factory was smoky and dark. Machines whined noisily in the machine shop. Kensington 'Kenny' C. Del Sol, a bearded and long-haired man of about 30, wearing dirty blue factory jumps and worn combat boots, looked at the calendar and the clock beside it clock. The calendar said 2049, if you were one of the few people who could read. The clock read 1:00 in the afternoon—two hours to go before he could go home and open a cold beer. It might be the Second World Depression, but you could still enjoy a few simple things in life.

Kenny wiped a sleeve over his forehead. It was too hot inside the factory. San Diego sweltered in a Santa Ana condition, with hot, dry winds rushing west from the desert pushing almost all humidity out into the sea. The air conditioning was broken, as usual. Nothing ever worked right. So much stuff was broken. The many broken cars, machines, old shoes, and what not created plenty of work for the many segments of Harrison Industries. But the company's main concentration, like much of the nation's, was the insatiable need for all sorts of defense industries. Night and day, the factories pumped out fighter planes, bombers, bullets, uniforms. Every tenth citizen was in the military. Everything else, from groceries to education, from healthcare to housing, took the back seat.

Grimy, with his hair hanging sweatily and his beard matted with flecks of oil, Kenny swept the shop floor with an extra-wide broom. He was new here, low man on the totem pole, just moved in from upstate New York, and checked in with San Diego Police to get his residence permit. Without that, you couldn't rent a shack, drive a car, or even buy a cup of coffee.

"Hey, Del Sol," called out his one new acquaintance, a big quiet man named George Beasley, who had a very scary gaze. Beasley was a senior machinist and really knew his stuff. Like the other men here, Beasley wore a dirty blue shop jumpsuit with torn sleeves and cuffs. He wore a pair of old, scuffed brown dress shoes with no laces, and no socks. Life was like that.

It was tough getting a new start. Something bad had happened in Albany, and Kenny had gotten away just in time. He couldn't remember what it was, but the police there would be looking for someone, and there were dead bodies involved. Whether he'd done something or not, he had no idea. But in today's world, even suspicion could land you in jail. At 32, Kenny wasn't old enough to remember anything about the Good Old Days that people talked about—when the lights always worked. When everyone had a car and a refrigerator, but nobody was happy. Everyone was angry all the time. They didn't know how bad things could get. The old folks talked about nothing else. Nobody dared talk about the Great Shepherd who kept America safe. It was okay to talk about the Good Old Days, because the Great Shepherd promised one day America would be rich and happy again. All other countries, those that survived the Big Meltdown, were in far worse shape after the economic catastrophe, and wars and diseases. Some places, like Canada and parts of Europe, were radioactive cesspools where weird and deformed creatures crawled around at night, trying to eat each other. The world had broken up into petty little kingdoms and dictatorships. Half of them were communist, the other half socialist. From what Kenny had learned over the years, there was little difference between the two. Both ways of thinking wanted to take bread off your table and give it to someone who didn't have bread because he was too lazy to earn any. Like most people, Kenny didn't have time for a lot of philosophy like that. He was too busy surviving from day to day. Somedays you had nothing to eat. Other days you had enough to eat double and make up for it. Most people figured—if you had shoes on your feet, and something to keep the rain off your back; if you had a full stomach and maybe a little beer for the evening ballgame at the tavern video show; and a warm, dry, safe place to sleep that night—what more did you need? Most people didn't have much, and there was a good deal of cooperation. Fear and hunger brought people together. Decent people, at least. There were always bad ones.

"Hey, Del Sol!" Beasley repeated.

Kenny looked around—was the foreman watching? It was easy to get in trouble and lose a shit job like this, and then what would he do? Satisfied he wasn't drawing any angry looks, Kenny pushed his broom down one oily concrete aisle, past the rubber extruders that smelled like cooking school gone haywire, took a right, and went to Beasley's corner with its complex machines.

"How you doing?" Beasley asked without looking at Kenny. He continued working on his numeric jigger.

Kenny kept moving the broom around without looking at Beasley." Good so far, today. How you been?"

"All right." Beasley pulled a battered, dirty data tablet from under his table and laid it on the corner of his steel work surface, out of the way. "This mean anything to you?"

Kenny looked around furtively and edged closer. On the display, facing up, was what looked like a copy of an old news clipping from when news came out on paper, in The Good Old Days. It was from page 16 of the San Diego Union-Tribune, dated 2010—seventy-four years ago. Had two grainy photographs. One was of a young man in some sort of uniform, looking off in one direction with that vague smile and pleased look people have in all-purpose photos. The other was of a pretty young woman with medium, straight hair, looking in another direction. She was also smiling vaguely and generically. The little headline read:

DEA Agent Missing, Presumed Dead in Bomb Attack; Wife Murdered by Presumed Mob Killers.

Kenny could read pretty well, unlike most people. He glanced through the article, looking for anything of interest to him, but there was nothing. A Drug Enforcement Agency (what was that?) Special Agent Joseph Mackinson, 32, was missing and presumed murdered because his car had been found at a stakeout site near Ocotillo Wells, burned out and partially melted as if hit by an incendiary bomb. At the same time, around ten p.m., unknown assailants, presumed to be U. S. thugs working for Mexican drug cartels, entered the agent's home and savagely butchered his wife, Carla, 27, in a revenge attack for a recent drug bust. The Medical Examiner said her body was so badly mutilated that she had to be identified from dental records.

"That mean anything to you?" Beasley repeated.

Kenny shrugged and shook his head. "Why are you showing me that? It's over seventy years old."

"Someone gave it to me, and said to show you." He replaced the tablet under the table with a wicked grin. "I was testing your reading skills, that's all. You're pretty good. Now get lost before we both get docked. Keep your distance from me."

A man at a nearby press machine made low warning whistle, signaling that a supervisor was prowling in the area. Kenny quickly pushed his broom down the aisle and looked busy. The foreman, Mr. Durango, passed by. Mr. Durango was a short, angry man with dark hair and a white shirt with sleeves rolled up over brawny, hairy arms. He had a heavy beard shadow. His face had a sweaty sheen that made his beard shadow glisten like gun metal. With him was a tall, gray man in his 70s, a ghost almost, wearing a business suit and looking god-like. That would be Mr. Harrison himself, from the photos Kenny had seen hanging in the front lobby. Mr. Harrison was said to be a trillionaire, with plants all over America, but he still inspected his factory floors regularly. The foreman looked nervous and gave Kenny a mean look. "Put some snap in it. You look like you're sleepwalking. We don't need workers who are slow and lazy."

"Yessir." Kenny nodded frantically and leaned into it, pushing the broom. He wasn't sure why he had such good reading skills. Illiteracy was said to be at 93%, since the digital advances since the 1990s had made it possible for most people to conduct their lives without needing to read or write. Icons were everywhere, as were holograms. Doors no longer read 'exit'—a computer avatar woman's comforting voice told you the door you were near was an 'exit' in a voice laden with nurturing. It was all so much warmer than the cold, disembodied, printed word. A simple message like 'this is the stairway to the second floor' could be rendered in voices and symbols so sexy and nurturing that you lingered to listen several times before venturing upstairs.

* * * *

There was a considerable promotional effort to make the Harrisons seem like a princely family, a Kennedy-like Camelot. Even in a democracy, the common people seemed to eat this up. There was a booming television industry devoted to following the rich and famous. The tone was reverent but inquisitive, respectful but confessional. The funeral of Joseph Harrison, Sr. had been a national event, with three days of mourning and long church services. Just thirty-three families of unimaginable, trillionaire wealth were now America's royalty, without anyone saying that.

There were nearly 1,000 other families in a second tier of wealth—the billionaire aristocracy, without anyone ever saying it out loud. The leader of the nation, the Great Shepherd (first among trillionaires, whose very name remained a secret, though he gave inspirational weekly broadcasts), was a remote figure who almost never appeared in the media glare. He was treated not only as President, but as a religious leader through whom God spoke directly to his people, the suffering, heroic, and enduring people of America.

Common people—in factories, on farms, in offices, in the home—could follow the exploits of Trent Harrison's extended family, who were active in sports, industry, education, philanthropy, religion, patriotic causes. The factory where Kenny worked was saturated with images of the Harrisons. The mostly illiterate workers, when on break, could touch these icons on the walls, and hear either prayers, or a story about the Harrisons. Each Harrison had that beneficent, kindly smile that was so reassuring.

One of Trent Harrison's brothers was a general in the Army of the Borders, manning the great siege wall, hundreds of feet tall in some places, that surrounded America and protected her from the hostile world beyond. Another of his brothers was a senator from Texas. A third brother was the leader of a Biblically Correct mega-church with over one million members linked together via televideo. A fourth brother had died years ago in an air raid by Canadian intruders. A sister was the executive director of American Christian Charities, which took in and fed impoverished city orphans, educated them in Bible verses, and gave them constructive work under dignified conditions in far-off places.

Trent Harrison, one of the nation's 33 trillionaires, was a tall, studious looking man. He looked ascetic, so thin was he. It was said he worried and cared day and night about the millions of average Americans who worked in his defense plants, continuing the work of keeping America safe in a world full of venomous enemies. Trent Harrison had four children. The oldest son, a clean-cut, somber looking man in his late twenties, was a student of Divinity in Mississippi. The younger son, a brighter, happier looking red-head with uneven teeth, was said to be grooming to take over Trent Harrison's place as Chief Executive Officer and President of Harrison Industries.

Then there was the older daughter, Cheryl, a bronze medalist in the American Olympics recently. She was a runner and swimmer, with a bright smile, short blonde hair, blue eyes, and a roundish, strong, streamlined face—a plain, fresh, scrubbed All-American beauty. Sometimes one saw a news video of Cheryl Harrison, like a princess in a long gown, attending some ball in Washington, D.C. in company of one or another of the young men who were scions of their own great families.

There was a darker, younger daughter, Melody, who had melancholy eyes and a wan smile. One did not often hear about Melody. Even the propaganda machine surrounding the Harrisons could not disguise the personalities of this family. Melody was a cipher.

People around town, in the factory, on the streets, spoke reverently of the Harrisons. After all, their jobs, their livelihoods, the well-being of their families, depended on Harrison Industries. What small cars a few people owned were usually Harrisons. When you got sick, you went to Harrison Hospital—though healthcare, like everything else in a nation beset by the Long War, was strictly rationed. What little there was was privatized, and administered by the Harrisons. As Trent Harrison sometimes liked to say, on the Roger Thomas Daily Chat and other shows, "We succeeded in slaying the monster of big government, a socialist horror. Now we have to continue fighting off the communists and other enemies of America from outside, who want to destroy our cities, poison our minds, and destroy our way of life."

The truth was, as Kenny could see in his own life and the people around him, you paid lip service to the system that controlled every aspect of your life, and secretly you did what you had to survive. If that meant having a forbidden second job, so be it. If it meant not paying taxes on your under the table income, that was a time-honored tradition. If you had a serious illness, and Harrison Hospital denied care, you searched for herbal and alternative medicines. Everything had its kind of balance, and so the world moved along.

* * * *

Each afternoon, the break whistle shrilled. Today, as usual, the men went into the lunch room with its orange and lemon colored plastic chairs and wooden tables. There they brought their snacks and sat listening to the Daily Chat with Roger Thomas. "Good afternoon, friends," said Roger Thomas of the friendly face and thick black hair combed up in a wave. Like most men of middle and upper classes, he wore the common white shirt and dark tie. "We'll talk with our guests in a few moments, but first the News Update. Good news in the North Dakota Regional Command. American troops repulsed a probing attack by Canadian irregulars, leaving nearly one hundred of the deformed uranium men dead. Three Americans were killed and six wounded, one critically. We pray for his survival. The Central Canadian Government has refused to apologize. President Shepherd said this morning that eternal vigilance is the price of liberty in a world that has reverted to the middle ages, all but here in America. The Magnum Line, the Great Wall surrounding our nation, is effective every day in protecting the homeland. On the Southern Wall, a truckload of illegal invaders was caught and the 79 men and women on board were taken to detention in the San Diego, where they will be processed for return to Mexico. All other regions and border sectors are reported to be secure." Thomas' voice broke as he said: "The Shepherd, our President Shepherd, has again reassured us that America's defensive strategy in the Magnum Line is working totally well. With over ten million men under arms, and the loyal American women supporting them as auxiliaries and helpmates on all our borders, America is secure again today. And, Mr. President, as one loyal American patriot who salutes you, I pledge that we will all remain alert and vigilant. We have your back, Great Shepherd." It was said the President had once rejected the notion of being called the Good Shepherd, because this was one of the titles of his Boss in heaven, who spoke through him.

The lunch room resounded with cheers. Men pounded their fists on the table. "Right on!" "Yeah!"

Tom continued his news program. "We have reports of a plague outbreak in France."

At the very mention of France, many men started booing. Someone yelled: "Serves them right. Let them all die." Another yelled: "Damn devils, they're all going to hell anyway."

"The crumbling French infrastructure has failed to provide medical care, but the death rate among French peasant farmers has been so intense that the disease appears to have outrun itself and arrested itself. The American Defense Health Administration reports it does not represent a danger on this country's soil. In Russia, there has been a coup d'etat in one of the rival capitals, St. Petersburg. Dmitri Valadin, a New All-Russia Communist, with the aid of several paratroop brigades, seized the capital and now appears to be enjoying total control of the media. There are reports of wide-spread executions as the new regime asserts total control. The rival presidency in Moscow issued a statement deploring what it called illegal balloting in the nation's northeast sector, and demanded a return to Moscow's jurisdiction. Although Siberia was conquered by China fifty years ago, there is a Russo-Siberian government in exile, which has thus far issued no formal statement on the situation in St. Petersburg.

"In Tokyo's limited elections, in a nation that has lost half its population in a famine, the newly resurgent Japan National Party claims a solid victory, placing a warlike premier in power. The White House has issued a statement warning the Japanese to restrain their bellicose, anti-American rhetoric." An empty milk carton flew in the air and struck the video screen. Men booed.

"Here is some dreadful news. Muslim extremists have bombed a Christian church in the Holy Land, killing over 100 Bible-fearing worshipers. Vatican collaborators are said to have helped the Mohammedan terrorists to infiltrate the Sunday morning service in one of Palestine's last remaining churches, inflicting heavy damage on the building. The State Department has called for all real Christians in the world to organize a crusade to retake the Holy Land. We are hungering for that, ladies and gentlemen, but America is a nation beset and attacked by radiation freaks, communists, socialists, illegal invaders, and other demons night and day. We are an island of sanity in a broken, medieval world that hates us. We first have to focus on securing our borders with the help of God, and then we can reclaim for civilization and Christ those lands that have fallen by the wayside.

"That's the world for now, ladies and gentlemen—a total mess as always. We have to keep America strong and independent. We are surrounded by enemies, and the threat level is orange today.

One nation, fifty sovereign states, with the freedoms we all cherish—freedom of speech, freedom of guns, freedom of religion. Above all, we have to fight the pestilence of socialism and communism that keeps threatening to creep in and undermine the greatest nation there is. The only free nation left on earth!" His voice rose to a hoarse shout. "There will be no damned socialism in my America!" Men in the break room shouted and banged on the table. It was a great release for them, Kenny thought. Thomas thundered: "Be free men—hang on to your precious freedoms!"

The video screen winked off. The foreman's annoyed voice crackled on the public address system. "You have five minutes to return to your stations. We are falling behind schedule, and any man who is a minute late will be docked an hour's pay for every minute lost. Let's get cracking, men. Let's pitch in for victory."

* * * *

After work, Kenny walked the three miles from Barrio Logan to his third floor walk-up in an ancient brick building in Golden Hills.

As he walked, government holograms would speak to him in slogans. Some also had signs next to them, stenciled in black letters on plain white cardboard, for the few citizens who could still read.

The hologram speakers were always either a white-haired man in a business suit, who looked like a preacher, or an attractive middle-aged woman in demure clothing, who looked nice but not sexy.

Work Makes Us Free, said the hologram man.

Productivity Is Your Concern, said the hologram woman.

Got The Time? Donate An Hour, said the hologram man— that was the famous campaign when threat levels were red, and the Great Shepherd asked people everywhere to step up war production and donate extra time.

Smoking Helps The Economy, said the holograms.

And this one, on the public library wall outside: *Say No To Big Government. Say Yes To Lots of Little Government.*

On the church across the street: *Faith, Not Reason. Trust the Shepherd.*

Down the street: *Be Free-Buy Guns.*

* * * *

The money Kenny saved on bus fare amounted to an extra meal or two over a week's time. Besides, the walk did you good. It wasn't quite as hot in late mid-afternoon, though the sidewalks still shone as if the heat trapped in them was glowing, and the silica used to make them two centuries ago glittered with diamond intensity. The building had once been a wealthy doctor's mansion. It was now subdivided into a warren of efficiency studios for artists from the city and poor workers from the barrio. As he came into the heights, Kenny could see the city skyline to the north—a lovely dream in the late sunlight, the afterglow of the Good Old Days that lasted more than a century and collapsed in the early 21st Century. To imagine the old beauty, you could squint a little, ignoring ragged spots like the copper spire that hung a bit sideways, the hole were a clock had been on a tower, and the black dots of missing windows. Some of the skyscrapers were still functioning, up to the tenth floor or so; they now had crank-windows. The air conditioning no longer worked in those huge buildings, and nobody today knew why you didn't just let a fresh breeze in. The Old People had done things in such complicated ways.

To the west, you could see the ruin of the great bridge. The Coronado Bay Bridge had lost its high span a generation ago because nobody could afford to keep up the paint and maintenance, so the bolts were rusting through. The middle span dropped during an earthquake. The city department that saw to such things no longer even existed. All these high places—the bridge, the skyscrapers—were now just roosting places for birds. Occasionally, someone still walked a mile up the bridge to jump, as they had during the Good Old Days. Kids often went up there to launch model airplanes and watch them sail away into the ocean, into the city, down into the barrio. Children still had their innocence. They could go fishing off the piers, run wild in the canyons, wander down miles of beach. There were fewer people, too, which made for lots of empty houses and ruined buildings. In some of these lived crazy men, who grabbed kids and took them into the dark places and they never came out again. The radio and video never talked about things like that. Society focused on helping the Great Shepherd lead America through these frightening and dangerous times, back to prosperity. Like the skyline, prosperity was a hope that never stopped being beautiful.

Kenny stopped at the library. Ignoring the download and tablet rooms, he went to the old print books in back, where almost nobody went these days. He wandered around the shelves in a cool haze and silence that was one of his favorite things in the world. The book section was small. Most people didn't read. They had tablets of all sizes on which they watched video or downloaded games to play. Who needed reading when all public instructions (Stop, Yield, Caution, Stairs, etc.) were either voice or holograph, always nice to look at and sounding sensuous. Stop was a hand upheld, Walk was a little white man, Go was a green arrow, all very clever.

Half this book room consisted of religious volumes approved by the city, which paid for them, after all, with tax money—Bibles, Book of Mormon, tracts, sanctioned philosophers, and so on. He wasn't interested. He craved the escape of dreamy books, fictions, fantasies. They were books that the Church and the Government frowned on, but they reluctantly permitted some of them to circulate. After all, so few people read, and these were old classics, so what was the harm? He ran his fingers over the worn spines of books he'd already read—*1984*, *Brave New World*, *The Iron Heel*, *It Can't Happen Here*, *The Man Who Was Thursday*, *Time Out Of Joint*, *The Crying of Lot 49*, *Fahrenheit 451*… and more, and more… and when he found one he'd put off reading, he excitedly took it to the checkout desk. The title was *Daybreak 2045*. The librarian was a stern, white-haired man with a red face and a certain bleak kindness. "Got your permit?"

Kenny showed him the plastic-coated card the police had issued him, entitling him to live in San Diego, rent here, work here, check out officially approved books, carry a gun if he wanted, and sit at restaurant counters. With this much control, it was a safe world except for the crazy people in haunted ruins, and the ever-present danger of murderous infiltrators from the outside world. It was a vast difference between that and the peace in this library. Kenny had once seen a girl walking down a sandy street on a hot day in Upstate New York. He was on his way home from work, that time. A crazy woman with a cleaver had come running out of a ruined warehouse, wearing only a ragged black dress. Didn't say a word, but ran full tilt up to the girl and swung at her. She slashed her time and again, and the girl collapsed in a lake of blood. Kenny ran to help her. The madwoman turned and slashed at him. She caught him across the forehead, and he went down in the dust. With fading eyes, he watched the woman laugh and skitter off. Like an insect, she scuttled on her hands and knees back into the dark of her lair until the next trigger would fire up her methed-out ganglia.

Kenny, standing in the library, jerked back with a sobbing breath. He almost dropped his book at the memory that had sneaked up on him. He would always remember the dead girl lying in her own blood. He remembered the woman's huge, crazed eyes, her meaty fingers on the handle of the cleaver, the mess of wet pink meat in her mouth as she came out with her epiglottis wriggling from all the ragged groaning, as in a low scream. He remembered her panting, too—out of breath, almost sexual in a craving to slice that sharp blade through human flesh, make blood spray everywhere, end a life there on the dirty street. Preachers said the meth-mad people were infested with demons, and they showed you Bible verses at Sunday sermon to prove it. They could prove everything they said from their Bibles. They could read. It was a powerful thing.

"That one's being withdrawn," the old librarian said, snatching the book away and hiding it under the counter. Just as quickly, he slid another out for Kenny to see. "Take this one. It's good."

"But I wanted that one," Kenny said in annoyance, thinking he might just reach over and grab his book back.

"Whizzago," said the old man. He snapped his fingers.

"Yessir," Kenny said, accepting the book. It had a plain brown case-bound cover, with the title pressed in gold leaf: *Leaves of Grass*. It was a book of poems. "Looks like a good one."

"You got a week with it," said the old man, shoving the book at him. His face looked stern but kind, and the combination made for a veiled meaningfulness that Kenny noticed but could not decipher. "You won't need more than that. Enjoy."

"Thank you, Sir." He forgot the old man as soon as he stepped into the hall and walked along the shaded, creaky wooden floor to leave the building. Children sat at tablets in the front rooms, engrossed in learning and games. The tablets didn't teach them to read anymore. Instead, it was all cartoon lessons, little squeaky pig voices that the kids laughed at while they watched Columbus sail the ocean blue in a cartoon ship, and animated Pilgrim Fathers praying as they shared a meal with pious-looking Squanto and his merry band of red-skins.

Kenny went two more blocks and stopped at the corner drugstore to buy a chilled beer in a bottle. He trudged up the dark wooden stairs that creaked under his tired boots. He rattled the key in the lock and entered his room. It was small, and you had to share a toilet down the hall, but it had a cot, a metal locker, and a little corner sink. With this heat, it was a good thing he had a north exposure, with a poor view, and no direct sunlight beating down. The window was open to a hot breeze that wheezed in and out. The window had a plastic curtain with big yellow fishes on it, that had been cut from an old shower curtain. If you lifted it, you could look out over a treetop at the windows of another former mansion, now also chopped up into a warren of dwellings. There were young women over there, and Kenny would have liked to enjoy watching them sunbathe on the grass in the backyard, but he worked twelve hours a day, five days a week, and eight hours on Saturday; and there was four hours of mandatory church on Sundays, which left little time for leisure. He dropped the curtain for privacy.

Kenny kicked his boots off and dropped his overalls on the floor. Welcoming the slight breeze ruffling the curtain, he lay on the bed in his underpants and a T-shirt. He held the cold bottle to his forehead a while and winked out into an exhausted doze. He dreamt he was running among ruins with dark doors. He woke up with a start as the beer bottle clunked to the floor. It didn't break, but the beer turned fizzy inside—a million frantic bubbles like tiny teeth, seething behind the glass. Kenny sat on the edge of the bed and watched the beer calm down. He went to the little sink and washed his face with a grimy washcloth that smelled of mildew. He laid the washcloth on the wooden window sill, where hot sunlight would purge it of demons. He washed his face with plain water from the single tap. The water was lukewarm, so baked was the ground it had run through in old cast-iron pipes to arrive here. He sat on the bed and carefully cranked the cap off the bottle. The beer had calmed down. He drank several big swigs and let the cool fizz invade his head. Some bubbles ran up his sinuses, and he choked up. He sneezed out some beer and coughed his bronchia clear. He almost laughed at the fun of it. It was like diving head-first into a municipal swimming pool, if you could find one, and getting cold chlorinated water up your nose. The beer drowned his smell-gland and made his head feel like it was in an alcoholic wheat field.

He went to his locker, and looked inside for a clean towel. There wasn't much—two clean, neatly folded white towels. And the grip bag with which he had hitch-hiked and ridden buses across country to get here. In the grip bag were odds and ends—his comb; his high school ring; a Gideon Bible he'd lifted in a hotel room and meant to read, trying to be a good citizen, but never had; a deck of playing cards; a Kraft envelope; and a few pencils and pens that looked very used. A mirror on the inside of the locker door showed him to be a somewhat bedraggled, light brown-bearded, and tousle-haired man with greenish-gray eyes. There was a faint, fine scar on his left cheek. He touched the scar and wondered about it. He took the ring out and looked at it. It was a very typical, ornate, heavy gold ring with a blue glass stone, and scrollwork that read St. Martin's on one side and H.S. on the other. He put the ring back and took out the envelope.

The envelope was addressed to Mr. Kensington C. Del Sol. No other writing, no sender. Kenny tore the gummed flap open and looked inside. There was one thing—a map. He pulled it out. It was a map of San Diego. He turned on the overhead bulb and stood under it to see better. He unfolded the map with a lot of rustling and crinkling and awkwardness. Why did he have a map of San Diego? He didn't remember buying one. He studied it for a good ten minutes. It was a fairly old map, and showed the city as it had been in the Good Old Days. There was Interstate 8 running east and west through Mission Valley, and Interstate 5 running north and south close to the beach. Each highway had a red, white, and blue shield with U.S. in it, and the number. But what was U.S.? What did that mean? Interstate must mean bigger than any one state, and that could only mean the Great Shepherd's government in Washington. Everyone called the nation 'America.' A lot of strange stuff on this map, especially buried in the fine print and the Legend. He noticed the neighborhoods had names. Growing tired, he folded the map away and turned off the overhead bulb.

He lay down and started reading. Oddly, the inside of the book was not Walt Whitman's *Leaves of Grass*. There were a few poems to make it look right to a casual reader, but starting around page 30 was another book where the rest of the poems should have been. The title page there said: *Hiking and Camping in Montana*. The author was some obscure college professor from that region. The publisher was a small press in Helena, Montana. Puzzled, Kenny flipped through the pages. He'd seen books like this—plain black and white pages, square maps with icons: squiggly lines for elevations, round shadings for high mountains, straight lines for main roads, lettering for towns. This must be a very old book, because nowadays you got a tablet book, where you still had some lettering, but the illiterate could touch the letters with a fingertip and hear a voice say the words. This was just a plain, old-fashioned book. He knew he must read it, so he started on page 30 and read. The descriptions were from long ago, and spoke of things he did not quite understand. What was a rest stop? Who was Smoky the Bear? What was a park ranger? What were Yellow Pages? He read bravely on until he fell asleep.

A knock on the door startled him, and he sat up abruptly. "Huh?"

He heard another knock. Heart pounding, he rose in the gloom and staggered to the door. His bare foot knocked over the beer bottle; hee heard a few last mouthfuls spill on the wood floor. "Damn!" He opened the door, standing modestly to one side, and looked out. There stood Beasley in the hallway, with a bare, low-watt bulb wrapping him in a beery glow. Beasley regarded him with those telegraphing eyes and that cold smile full of dark intentions, all of it unreadable. Beasley had changed into jeans, a white T-shirt that revealed a tautly muscled upper body, and a brown baseball cap with blue and white logo HB. Under that it said Helena Brewers."Were you asleep?"

Kenny yawned and nodded. He ran a hand over his rumpled hair and tugged at his beard.

"Whizzago," said Beasley, and snapped his fingers. "When the Postman comes, call me." He handed over a medallion as large as a $5 dollar coin, with the same round shape, but some government slogan printed on it, with an image of George Washington on the other side. "Just squeeze it three times, and I'll get the signal. Put that in your pocket and keep it with you. Trust me—your life depends on it. Now go back to bed."

Kenny closed the door. He lifted his dirty overalls from the floor and put the coin in their pocket. He tumbled back into bed, where he slid into a deep and dreamless sleep.

8. Korporate Freedomz

In the morning, he washed his dirty jumpsuit and left it to soak in the sink. He would hang it up in the hot sun when he returned from work, and it would be dry in an hour. That saved a quarter to wash at the Mr. Bubbles Automat. He opened a small can of bland army rations from his locker and ate his breakfast cold. He didn't care to eat cold things, but such were the times. For supper, he could put a can on the window sill and let the sun cook it.

From his window, the morning looked foggy and cool—rather a nice change, and great for walking to work. By midmorning, the marine layer would bake off, and the sun return. This fog probably meant that the Santa Ana was over and the daily marine layer was back. He cleaned up the beer stain on the floor, and put the empty bottle in the little trashcan under the sink. He flipped the curtain up over the rod, so that air and light could freely circulate and take out the slightly stale, sweaty smell. Dressed in fresh overalls, he headed off to work. His mind was partly on the tour guide of Montana, partly on hoping he'd make it until payday with the $18 in his wallet, and partly on whatever interesting this or that passed him on the street. There were the usual slogans, the pretty women, the passing armored vehicles in which loomed shadowy, dark, bulletproof-vested police. Most of the police armored cars had a machinegun turret on top, manned by a policeman with white helmet.

As usual, there were few cars on the crumbling streets. People kept old cars patched, some fifty years old, but there were frequent shortages of hydrogen fuel. Unemployment was high. People survived by going under the radar, working under the table, and bartering on the black market. At least a quarter of the American economy was the shadowy underwater part of the iceberg. The so-called brand-name economy sold American-made goods to Americans only, behind the Border Wall that ran nearly 12,000 miles around the contiguous lower 48 states. The Border Wall was at least 100 feet high and topped with loops of concertina wire that carried a high voltage to kill any living thing that touched it. Behind the Border Wall, or Magnum Line, was the millions-strong

Army of the Borders, distributed in 1,984 command posts from Florida to Maine, from Maine to Washington State, from there to San Diego, and from San Diego to Key West. Cameras and sensors were everywhere, and the slightest motion could invite a drone, or a helicopter, or a ground patrol. It was totally privatized, like everything else, and the Great Shepherd had once said it was 20% of the Gross Domestic Product. It was Business, and that was good for America.

He passed a slogan that read: *Better Dead Than Red.*

Kenny was jolted out of his reverie by a loudspeaker. "Citizen, stop." He stopped and looked at the police cruiser that had pulled up on the street near him. Two armed men in dark Kevlar armor and white helmets climbed out. A third man on top manned the roof gun. A fourth man was on the microphone inside the blocky van, continuing to give instructions. "This is a routine check. Nothing to be alarmed about. Turn and face the wall."

Kenny faced a brick wall on which vandals had made looping, cryptic scrawls of graffiti in white spray paint. On the wall above him, the attractive but not sexy hologram woman appeared briefly and said: *Live Free or Die.*

"Place your hands on the wall where we can see them, and spread your ankles apart." Kenny wasn't quite fast enough, and a steel-toed boot kicked first one heel, then the other, to spread his legs so he had to lean on the wall for balance.

"With one hand, slowly reach for your Citizenship Permit and take it out for an officer to inspect."

Kenny pulled out his wallet and started to open it with both hands.

"Keep your right hand on the wall," one officer said sharply, and Kenny did so.

The other officer took the wallet from Kenny's left hand, and extracted the card. Kenny watched through a corner of his eye as the card went under a gun-like scanner that analyzed all data on a chip buried in his photo.

"Turn your head to the left," said the man in the car.

Kenny complied, and the scanner-gun analyzed his facial features to compare with the photo. "Okay, pal," said the policeman. He stuffed the wallet carelessly into Kenny's pocket, which was unpleasant and invasive. He didn't like the man's touch, and wished he could hit him. He bit his lip and suppressed the urge, knowing it would end grievously for himself if he resisted.

The loudspeaker said: "Put both hands on the wall and remain there until we signal you can go. Congratulations, Citizen. Your papers were found to be valid."

Car doors slammed, and the vehicle drove off. Halfway down the block, the siren emitted a brief phhhwwweeeet!, signaling he was free to continue on his way. When he looked in his wallet, he counted $12 in bills. They'd taken most of his singles, leaving two fives and two ones. There was no way to fight it, so he resolutely kept walking. He was glad it had ended peacefully, and it looked as if he was really under the radar. That much was great in itself. Those cops, running their wireless check-scans as they had, would have instantly known if there were any warrants for his arrest from New York State and its subdivisions.

* * * *

George Beasley, the machinist with the Helena Brewers baseball cap, never even glanced in Kenny's direction that day at work. Kenny thought it best to avoid him. He thought of him as an acquaintance, certainly, not a friend, but he also didn't trust him. Kenny did not have any friends here in San Diego yet.

Other than being searched on the street from time to time, his life stayed peaceful. He knew someone—the superintendent, the police—entered his room from time to time and looked around, when he was not at home, but it was so stealthy and unobtrusive he almost didn't mind. Nothing had been stolen, yet, and there was nobody to complain to, so why be bothered? He swept and cleaned with vigor at work. Each Friday, he got his pay as he left work. At $4 an hour minimum wage, he received $276 for a 68-hour work week, which included a $4 stipend for korporate mandated church attendance—four hours on Sunday mornings. That left $1,100 a month for rent ($500) rent and weekly expenses ($150).

You could get by on minimum wage if you weren't married and had no dependents or health issues. Kenny had no health insurance and could never see a doctor or dentist, but he'd been lucky so far and was in good health. If you went to the E.R., they read you your 'Christian Rights' and patched you up, a one-time visit for any specific illness. You still got a hefty bill from the private insurance company that paid the hospital corporation. After that, you were on your own, and many people turned to faith healers, herbal doctors, and other off-the-grid remedies. In the Good Old Days, there had been some limited programs called Social Security, Medicare, and what not, but that had all been abandoned as the economy shrank, and government abandoned more and more sectors under pressure from the Great Shepherd and the large corporations.

Only Big Business Can Save Amerika Now, was one slogan of The Shepherd's party. More and more holograms opened to briefly speak, all around the city streets:

Big Government is Godless Communism.

Big Business is Good Business.

Health Care Run by Big Government Is A Heartless Socialist Scam.

Don't Let Big Government Take Your Freedom of Choice Away.

The Business of Big Business Is Your Health.

Capitalism Is The Faith Of Good Christians.

Big Business is God's Business.

9. Talmadge

During the break on Friday, Kenny and the others received free coffee and donuts and watched old family home movies of the Harrisons. Cheryl really was a beautiful girl, maybe sixteen at the time, standing with her ascetically smiling father and her beautiful mother. The film must have been made some years ago, because the two boys were still teenagers, and Melody was an adorably dimpled, smiling like girl with glossy brown ringlets, sitting on a rocking horse with her big sister Cheryl protectively hovering around her. Cheryl always hovered over her little sister.

Kenny and Beasley avoided each other. Kenny glanced over once, and saw Beasley humming to himself as he measured something with an electro micrometer. Then Beasley glanced toward the office with that crazy look that scared Kenny. Kenny bent over his broom and pushed as hard as he could, so that spiral tin shavings, misfit nuts and bolts, and a thick coating of black, oily dirt moved before him.

After work, Kenny clomped up the stairs, entered his room, and took his boots off. As he sat on the cot, tugging at a boot, he noticed a multicolored paper, the size of a playing card, by his side on the dark army blanket. Had it fallen from his pocket? Had someone put it in his pocket or brought it to the room?

He picked up the card, looking at its front and back. The issuing authority read San Diego Metropolitan Transit System. He held here a one-day bus pass good to the end of 2049. Once you started using it, you could ride as far and as long and as often as you wanted, but it was only valid for 24 hours from the first usage stamp. After washing his face and neck with tap water to cool down, Kenny thought of something. He went to the locker, and took the map from his grip bag. He turned on the overhead light and spread the map out on the bed. Someone had gone into the locker and used one of his pencils to mark up the map. He was sure of it—and it had to be the same person who had left the bus ticket. Those two circles had not been there before. He had a deep, wrenching feeling in his gut. He almost felt like violently heaving. Something black and horrible was thrashing in his soul, like a crocodile disturbed in the deep water and lashing around for life and death.

* * * *

On Saturday, after work, Kenny took a bus ride. He had the map in his pocket. He was still wearing his dirty overalls. He was sweaty, and didn't like to be on a bus dressed like this, but he had no choice. Several nicely dressed older ladies avoided sitting near him. In frustration, he rose and went to sit in one of the rear corners, where he almost had to bend his head forward because the curving ceiling. The air conditioning on the bus was broken, but it had forced air, and that made for some cooling. He leaned his head tiredly against the window and yawned. The bus, fueled with hydrogen in a cell on top, trundled from stop to stop, from Golden Hill to North Park, onto El Cajon Boulevard. It went down the Texas Street hill into Mission Valley, where Kenny got out at an ancient shopping mall, now mostly boarded up and with ceilings falling in. He boarded a No. 13 bus that would take him the rest of the way. It was still a long ride, and he grew more tense, more dreading, more filled with anticipation and almost fear. The bus roared along the city streets in the San Diego River valley.

There must have been a massive waterway, millions of years ago, to carve out a vast canyon like Mission Valley, Kenny thought, but now the river was a shallow waterway averaging twenty feet across. Six or seven miles from the ocean, the river was choked up with tall reeds and gloomy oaks, under which many homeless families lived. Only at its delta did it grow to about two hundred feet as it swilled slowly into the Pacific Ocean.

The bus swung through one small community after another: a business park; a strip mall with apartments; a poor neighborhood with cars up on concrete blocks and dirty kids screaming at stickball; a subdued college neighborhood; a bunch of dentist offices shaded by big willow trees; an old Catholic church with a pale Virgin Mary in a wall niche, spreading her arms in blessing over colorful flowers; a street of used car dealers; an Asiatown that smelled of frying noodles, fish, and hot peanut oil; on and on, in a whirl of constant change from one focus to the next. It became impossible to believe there could be more, but there always was.

The bus stops began to seem repetitious, as if he were traveling between parallel worlds, but he knew that was silly. He opened the map against and studied it. He sat with one foot raised on the broken air grating by the wall, the other stretched under the seat before him. There were only a few older men and women scattered about the fifty-something seats. Someone had made two circles on the map. One was Kensington. The other was Colina Del Sol.

His name—Kensington C. Del Sol. *How odd.*

His eyes fell on the neighborhood between them. *Talmadge. Huh?*

He studied the map repeatedly There were a bunch of wiggly little lines all over the map, representing neighborhoods. Where the unknown person was calling his attention tothree adjoining neighborhoods: Kensington, Talmadge, and Colina Del Sol.

That name Talmadge had some meaning but he had no idea what. The meaning was fierce inside of him, like a wounded animal trying to burst out of a cellar. The animal thrashed and howled in grief and loss. In rage and helplessness. What did it all mean? Stunned, he got off and boarded a #11 bus that took him through Talmadge, from Kensington to Colina Del Sol. What mystery was trapped here as the sun hung dying in orange agony in the sweltering western sky? He sat there not knowing why, and cried like a baby. Tears flowed from his eyes and fell on the map, so that it grew soggy and disintegrated between his helplessly clawing fingers. He cried and cried all the way into Colina Del Sol, where he got off the bus. People were used to anything these days, and ignored him. He wandered west, still crying, on El Cajon Boulevard for miles, like a crazed homeless man, until he got to 70th Street and remembered his pass was good into the next day. He felt weak, wrung out, dehydrated. He washed his face at a gas station toilet, and drank from the tap. As the last orange fire faded in the western sky, and darkness set in among the sparse city lights, he used his pass to ride a bus the rest of the way home.

Mouth
of God

10. The Postman Calls

On Saturday afternoon, as Kenny was leaving the factory, the foreman who sometimes yelled at him, Mr. Durango, called him over to his office. Kenny started to sweat. Had he done something wrong? Were they firing him? Mr. Durango looked rather furtively left and right, pulled Kenny into the office, and locked the door.

"Whizzago," said Mr. Durango as he pointed to a chair in the waiting room. Kenny felt himself grow a little weak for a second. There was a round table with magazines. The walls were covered with Harrison family pictures—Trent Harrison, his beautiful wife, their two sons, their daughters Cheryl and Melody. In the room were three plain wooden doors, each painted the same bilious light green as the office itself. Each door had a tag pasted to it: Office, Reception, and Toilet.

Kenny sat on one of six wooden, high-backed chairs with armrests. "I am the Postman," said Mr. Durango. Kenny put his hands in his pockets, felt the medallion, and secretly squeezed it three times. It led out a brief tingle of warmth to let him know his message had been transmitted.

"What am I supposed to do?" Kenny asked.

"You can stop being dumb, for one thing." Durango's powerful, compact body arched and he snapped his fingers several times. His gunmetal cheeks gleamed. "I'm releasing you from the lowest layer of your program. We need you, Kenny."

"I'm ready to do what I can."

"Good."

Kenny heard a toilet flush. The door opened, and out came Mr. Harrison, the trillionaire, zipping the fly of his three-piece charcoal business suit. He wore the prescribed white shirt and a merlot tie with a silver Harrison Industries tie pin. He was a tall, ascetic looking man with tanned, wrinkled skin and short graying hair parted on one side. He looked at Kenny, and then at Durango. "Is this the man?"

Durango nodded. "Yes, Mr. Harrison. We will travel together."

"Does this man understand the implications?"

"Nossir. Do you want to tell him?"

"You can explain when we are in the car."

At Durango's signal, Kenny followed his foreman out into the factory and downstairs to the garages. They walked a long way, through a gloomy atmosphere that smelled of oil and tires, amid darkly gleaming company cars and trucks. Eventually they reached a separate, executive underground garage area below the office where Kenny had seen Harrison come out of the toilet. Kenny was still a bit muddled, but at least now he knew someone had caused him to be muddled. He knew he was twenty intelligence points higher than he'd been this morning, but a certain sense of blockage, like internal walls, told him he was still missing a large part of his knowledge. He also knew, as with the cops frisking him and shaking him down, that he had no choice but to go along with the program.

As Kenny and Durango entered the carpeted executive garage—which Kenny hadn't dreamed existed, and he was sure few or none of the factory floor people did—Durango told him: "If we all do our part, this will go off without a hitch. I trust that they vetted you well."

"I have no idea what you mean."

Durango crossed the small underground garage, which was well lit and cleaner than the high-wear factory garage. There was an administrative office behind glass windows in one corner, but the lights were out and it appeared to be locked. Durango used a combination lock to open a thick steel locker. Inside were rifles and handguns, as well as olive green ammo pouches, all very new and neatly organized. Durango handed Kenny a nylon web belt that carried pouches for extra clips, as well as a black Glock automatic in a nylon holster. "Here, put this on over it to hide it." He handed Kenny a large, loose blue work shirt. "Don't worry. Nobody is going to mess with Mr. Harrison and his brother. They're insiders." He pointed to the gun. "You should be handy with that. You were trained with it."

"Insiders?" Kenny asked as he buckled the belt and gun on. What did he mean, trained?

"Mr. Harrison is one of the 33 wealthiest men in the country. He controls health care rationing, automobile manufacturing, and other vital industries. He's a trillionaire."

"And you, Mr. Durango?"

Durango clapped a powerful hand, painfully, on Kenny's shoulder. "Listen, my friend. We don't have time for idle conversation and a lot of destructive questions. You won't be coming back here, so I can tell you a few things that will help you understand what we're doing. I'm an agent of POSENT. Nobody knows that but you and I. Let's keep it that way. Keep your mouth shut. These paranoid idiots might think it's something French or Liberal or whatever. You don't know what POSENT means. Don't worry about it. I'm from outside, in the future. We have Mr. Harrison's brother going with us as well. He'll be here in a minute. Help me load the ammo." He pointed to a black, boxy van with Army of the Borders plates. The van looked massive. It had sloped, bullet deflective surfaces all around, and small windows of thick glass. There were even gun ports to shoot from. Durango loaded several high-powered assault rifles into the back. Kenny carried two heavy ammunition cases to the van and heaved them in.

Durango grinned. "You'll enjoy the ride, my friend. This thing has jet engines for riding on the mega-highways in the sky. You'll get a taste for how these people live." He put a finger over his lips to urge silence and discretion.

Harrison came from one direction, and a man who looked a lot like him from another. Both men wore similar conservative clothing. They seemed personable enough, Kenny thought. They shook hands with Durango and Kenny, and got into the back seat. Durango drove, and Kenny rode shotgun.

The driver's cage was separated from the passenger cage in the rear by thick glass windows. That window remained sealed, affording the passengers in back total privacy. It also meant that the men in front could speak freely.

The garage doors rattled open and the car rolled forth. The car went up an incline while the door rolled shut behind them. "You'll have some questions," Durango said, "and I'll tell you what I can. Basically, Mr. Harrington is defecting to Canada."

Even Kenny, who couldn't care less, was shocked.

"That's a big deal if it gets out, obviously. In fifty years of the Great Shepherd State of America, there has never been a trillionaire openly defecting from this huge cashbox they've been looting for over many generations. I don't care about them one way or the other. I'm just interested in the City of En surviving. You'll know what that means when this mission is done and you go back."

"You said I wasn't coming back," Kenny said, not understanding.

"I said you were going back, not coming back. You'll be finished." There was a hidden, ominous edge that Kenny just barely caught. Durango's eyes flicked aside as if he weren't being entirely honest. Kenny had never liked him. You couldn't like a man who had a habit of yelling at you.

"So where do I go?"

"Back where you came from."

"Where is that?"

"Time Town! You ask a lot of questions."

Kenny digested that. Had he just exclaimed in frustration when he yelled Time Town, or was that a place? He decided not to press.

"Harrison's got his reasons. He says it's for the good of America. That's his brother with him, a general in the Army of the Borders. That's why nobody is going to question us as we go through the border zone. They're defecting together. Personally, I think they power structure is forcing Harrison out. He's one of the ruling elite. I think there's a power struggle going on among the predators at the top."

"You mean Washington, D.C.?"

"That's just where they keep up the pretense of democracy. That's where the talking goes on. Their real power base is spread around, like the ducal system in Europe. Some have their base in New York City, or Chicago, or Atlanta—you name it. You can certainly call men like Harrison dukes or grand dukes or whatever. The Great Shepherd is their king. Some big cities have two or three dukes. Most have one. "

"How do they keep the system going?"

"It evolved, same way it does in all places in all times. More and more power concentrated in fewer people. They control the media and rule by lies and fear. To really control information, they've created this phony war between America and the rest of the world."

"You mean the U.S.? What is the U.S.?"

"Was. It's now the Great Shepherd State, with very little government, everything privately run by the Big Corporations. It used to be a federal system called the United States of America, based on a constitution written in 1787. There were checks and balances on everyone to prevent any one person from having too much power. That didn't last. It didn't suit the big corporations, who want freedom from rules so they can do whatever they want. No government, no oversight. They harnessed the information flow by owning the media, so they could lie and distort the truth, and create constant hysteria. Fear and guilt are the two big controls. The other threat was from popularly elected representatives. So they shaped who would be elected by using the media and rumor mills in the information networks. Lying to the population, keeping them ignorant and in fear, and in a state of religious terror all at the same time. And there were outside enemies, terrible ones with great fangs and teeth. Gradually, it came to this point where they have the whole country living in poverty, hiding behind their great wall, and building weapons for a totally unneeded defense industry. It's become a nightmare state in which everything is the opposite of what is said. The people were turned into their own worst enemies, without even realizing it, and they suffer terribly. The people are angry, hurt, and confused. If they weren't lied to constantly, they would see who has done all this to them—the huge corporations."

"I hope they can't hear us back there," Kenny said.

"Doesn't matter. The Harrisons are defecting to the outside world. We'll help them." He continued his explanation. "The corporations kept working insidiously to change from a federal system, with centralized rules and controls. They began using the idealistic name, America, and dropped the U.S. Now it's more of an idealist, religious dictatorship run by the Great Shepherd. That's how it all started, in New England, hundreds of years ago, with strict religionists who hated the British Crown, so in their hearts, a lot of these people yearn for that. They also happen to have the most powerful military in the world, so the military-industrial-religious-media nexus is all-powerful. With the government and the population totally under control, that leaves the dukes to fight among each other. I think they're forcing Harrison out, meaning either to kill him or force him to retire to a ranch, and he's choosing to defect to those horrible enemies in Canada, on the other side of the Great American National Border Wall."

"I'm just here as added muscle?" Kenny felt intimidated by the scope of what Durango had been explaining.

"Yes. You have the training we need for the person slated to fill this position. You happened to come along, as the right person at the right time. From what they tell me, it wasn't planned. It was just a rolling opportunity, and someone high up made a field decision. Piece of cake, pal."

After a while, Durango said: "You can get some sleep if you want."

"Thanks, I might doze off a bit."

"Are you hungry?"

"I'm always hungry, Mr. Durango."

"There's food in the cooler at your feet." He laughed.

Kenny leaned down and opened the dented blue-white plastic cooler. There, in a bed of ice cubes, were sandwiches in waterproof boxes. There were also bottles of cold coffee, juices, and colas. "I'll eat after I sleep. You're laughing."

"I am. Sorry. You've been with those poor shits long enough to start hoarding food and saving on bus fare and all the rest of what they have to do to stay alive. Yes, they were great once, but so were the Romans and the British."

"I see." He knew vaguely of Romans and British—he'd heard of these long-ago nations somewhere. No idea where or when. He liked Durango less and less. Something about the man was offensive. He shut him out and closed his eyes. As he dozed off, he wondered about that remark about saving bus fare. It sounded as if Durango had been spying on him. But then, that was logical, given that he had been set up for this mission.

When he woke, the car was on a mega-superhighway in the air. The car was flying along, so to speak, at hundreds of kilometers per hour on one of the modern Highways of the Air. "Hello," Durango said quietly. He had soft classical music playing, and a steaming black coffee at his side. "Coffee maker is under the dash. Help yourself."

"Thanks." Kenny sat back and enjoyed a ham and cheese sandwich, a banana, a cup of coffee, a small vanilla pudding. He washed it all down with a second cup of coffee. He enjoyed the flow of traffic on the forty-lane mega-highway a thousand feet in the sky. The lights were beautiful, as were the plush interior of the car, and the classical music. "How much longer?"

Durango looked at his dials. "We're doing four hundred miles an hour, and we've been on the road for two hours, so I'd guess another six hours in all. This road doesn't go all the way to the Canadian border. We get off and take older roads." Durango reached behind himself and opened a panel in the space between their seats. He pulled out some heavy clothing. "It's going to be cold where we are going. I think it's about ten degrees Fahrenheit. You better think about putting these on over your clothes."

Kenny reached over to take the thickly padded field jacket Durango was offering him amid an armload of other clothing. As Kenny dug his hands into the pile, he noticed something hard and floppy. Durango noticed, and pulled at his own segment of the pile. Then Durango pushed Kenny's pile toward him, and pulled his own toward himself. As Kenny sorted through his jacket and over-pants, he mulled over what had just happened. A strange thought bubbled up. Durango's field jacket had bullet proof shielding in it, and Durango was making sure Kenny got one without shielding. He didn't trust this situation any further than he could throw Durango, which was about nil.

11. The Magnum Line

The car descended smoothly along a series of exit lanes, until they were driving on a normal super-highway from the Good Old Days. It was still an impressive road, and the dukes maintained it well.

In places, ice rattled against the window. Freezing grit blew up under the car. Ice flowers formed on the glass.

The inside plate window whined as someone in back lowered it. Harrison's voice sounded forth. "We're getting close, I see."

"Yessir, about another half hour we are on the other side."

"Excellent," said the general, also a Harrison. "You men have done your job well. I think it's going to go without a hitch. There will be a nice reward for each of you. Here is the first part." He reached forward with a gray-gloved hand that reeked of wealth, and handed Kenny a dark-blue leather wallet. Kenny looked inside and saw several hundred dollar bills. General Harrison handed a similar wallet to Durango, who pocketed it with thanks. Durango joked warmly: "Sir, I feel like a limo driver getting his tip. Thank you so very much."

"My pleasure," said the General, warmly.

"And mine," said his brother, warmly. Money made the world go round. These men had been born to princely power and were relaxed about their omnipotence. They were comfortable chatting lightly with ordinary mortals, whom they could just as easily order killed, imprisoned, or tortured, simply by a whispered word to an aide.

The General spoke on a telephone, and didn't seem at all worried or upset at leaving his homeland forever. He even laughed and joked. "Okay, dear. Okay. I'll see you soon, honey. We'll celebrate." Kenny didn't mean to, but he glanced back into the richly appointed bar and sleeper in back. General Harrison was smiling. He winked. "My wife. You know how it is."

Kenny looked away, not sure what to say. So he said nothing. He didn't really know how it is.

"Mr. Durango, you can relax," the General said. "I just spoke with the Field Duty Officer at the Milk River Sector on the Magnum Line. I've been through here many times, and they won't think anything unusual. It will be important, on your return trip, that you keep the rear section here dark as if we are in it. Slow down for the checkpoint coming this way. The Canadians won't give you any trouble. Our people are all fangs and teeth, but they wouldn't stop my car. Just slowly drive through and head back into America as if nothing had happened."

Durango said: "Yessir. I'll do exactly that."

Kenny thought to himself, what about all the monsters, the radiation swamps, the terrible enemies?

The Great Wall loomed ahead, a black strip across the brightness that radiated behind it. It was a hundred feet tall here, equivalent to a ten-story building. A row of American flags fluttered on top, amid endless coils of accordion wire. This was officially a National Monument, besides all else, and special rules applied here. Stubbornly, the Stars and Stripes were kept illumined and hoisted night and day to threaten America's enemies that lurked everywhere.

As the car slowed down, Kenny saw that the ten miles immediately behind the wall were a great industrial zone supporting the entire defensive wall. There were complexes for harnessing geothermal energy and driving the great ring of lights that shone all night and on cloudy days to prevent real or imagined infiltrators. The military garrisons had their housing, their shopping complex, their hospital, their every need met here in the wilderness far from most American cities. The Wall, all privatized, took a great chunk of GDP and was probably the biggest single operation in the entire defense industry.

Kenny was puzzled at the sight of wraiths wandering around in snowy, barren fields in the middle of nowhere—thin people with large, scared eyes, who looked as if they were starving and freezing. "Who are they?" he asked.

Durango made a 'shut up' face, jerked his eyeballs as if pointing toward the rear, and punched Kenny furtively on the thigh, so the men in back wouldn't notice the gesture.

They drove through checkpoint after checkpoint. Armed and helmeted guards waved the general's slowly moving vehicle through. If Durango had any comments, he was keeping his mouth shut because of the open window behind him. Kenny could read between the lines and understand that people like the Harrisons were above the law. While people wandered around, starving, behind their great defensive walls, their rulers were in the habit of regularly driving into Canada.

The road narrowed down to two lanes—one coming, one going—and dipped down into a concrete barrel that ran underground. From the signs and equipment all around in the brightly lit industrial tunnel, Kenny could guess that, in theory, the tunnel could be instantly flooded with water if an invading army were coming this way. There was no end to the paranoia, and the billions of dollars spent fueling it on both the supply and demand ends.

The car sailed along, rising from the ground. It slowed as it emerged into the more natural night air on the other side, a softer air not swimming in frosty artificial light. Now it was West Canadian flags that fluttered in the air: white, with the red maple leaf in the center, and two narrower, vertical red border stripes at each side. The West Canadian military and police were surprisingly a small presence. Unlike the descriptions of horror that Kenny heard in the Great Shepherd's broadcasts and those of anchors like Tom Rogers on his Daily Chat, there were no monsters or radiation mutants crawling around glowing in the dark.

Instead, Durango drove on brightly lit, modern highways toward a remarkable source of soft light on the horizon. The lighting there was not harsh and neurotic, but gentle and soothing. The signs read: Torquay, Canada's Shopping City. The roads in the city flowed with gleaming new cars, despite the late hour. The atmosphere was wealthy, serene, at ease with its glamor and power. Tasteful neon signs winked on and off on the streets. Music leaked from passing cars, nightclubs, street singers. Durango explained that the city was covered by a mile-high bubble of what appeared to be ultra-powerful, ultra-lightweight, transparent polymer glasstic. That meant it could be climate controlled from inside, and its waste products could be processed without much effect on the environment. In the balmy air, Kenny rolled down his window, which still had dirty, melting ice flowers on it.

"Stop here," said the general at a small, green park surrounded by a shopping plaza. "We'll waste no time, nor detain you."

"Thank you, and God speed," said Harrison as he and his brother got out.

Harrison leaned into the open window. "You men did your jobs. Thank you." He handed each their final monies, in two paper envelopes. Kenny and Durango both thanked him profusely.

Seeing the wonder—smelling leather, fine clothing, perfume, flowers, wonderful food as nice looking, healthy men and women bustled past—Kenny thought: I never want to go back to the poverty and the insanity. He watched the two men meet their wives, smiling, as they all linked arms. Probably going out for a fine steak dinner, Kenny thought. Probably cost what I make in a month or more.

"Don't think about bolting," Durango said in a slow, smug voice. "Your contract still needs to be fulfilled. You don't want to jeopardize that."

"You said I wasn't going back." Kenny rolled up the window as Durango pulled out through traffic and headed back south toward America.

"You have one more piece to fulfill and then you're done."

"Where are you taking me?"

"Back to America. That was Part One. Now for Part Two."

Seeing the Great American National Border Wall looming up, with American flags like a row of teeth on top, Kenny thought: Mr. Shepherd, tear down this wall.

The car rolled through the Canadian checkpoint, where leisurely border guards waved it through. Durango drove back through the tunnel, where he did as Harrison had instructed. He rolled slowly through each heavily fortified checkpoint, where scared men with machineguns sat, ready to start shooting. They recognized the car, and rifle-toting Army of the Borders troops saluted and waved them through.

In less than thirty minutes, they were out of the ten mile border-industrial zone and picking up speed. They came to a wide stretch of frozen snow that glittered like bluish ice cream under a full moon in a hazy, black sky. It was a desolate and beautiful sight. The road was still a two-lane straight shot without streetlights. Once in a while, Kenny saw more of those wide-eyed wraiths wandering in search of food and warmth. Some looked unnaturally small.

Every so often, Kenny thought he glimpsed a pair of headlights far behind them.

At a slight height overlooking snowy fields for miles around, Durango slowed the car. He pulled onto the shoulder, with ice crunching under the wheels. "Need to take a leak."

As Kenny waited, Durango got out and closed the door. He took the key with him, ever thinking ahead. He walked carefully over the ice, and disappeared into darkness around the rear. With the engine off, cold started seeping into the cab. Kenny decided he had to go too, and climbed out. As he stood overlooking a ditch, drizzling into the snow below, a light wind whipped his collar like knives of cold. He started shivering and couldn't wait to hoist his fly up and get back into the car. "Hey Durango," he called into the darkness. No sign of the man. Wind whispered in the fields as Kenny zipped up and started to turn.

"Stop right there."

As Kenny turned, he saw Durango aim a gun at him across the hood. He must have doubled around in the dark, and sneaked up from the other side of the road. He leaned his bulk over the hood and rested his elbows on the metal as he held the gun with both meaty fists. "Part Two, pal. Keep your hands in the air."

"I don't understand." Kenny raised his hands.

"I know. But I do. My orders are to kill you. That's the second little tweak. I don't know what you are up to, but it seems your life takes another few hours from my city. That's what the CloudMaster calculator hulks are telling us, and I just follow orders."

Out of the corner of his eyes, Kenny saw the distant headlights wink out as a car came toward them. Why would someone turn out their headlights just now? The distant car seemed to have stopped moving.

"Don't try to stall," Durango said. "I take no pleasure in this. I'll tell you what. I'm going to give you…" He raised his wrist and looked at his watch…"One more minute to live. How's that for a good thing. Enjoy yourself. Taste the air. Feel the cold. Look up at the stars. Love the snow." He started laughing coldly as he pulled back the gun's chambering mechanism. The click sounded loud in the cold air that moaned over the road face. Kenny could hear the copper-jacketed round slide through lightly oiled steel and into the rear of the barrel.

Kenny thought about throwing himself backward into the ditch. He must do something, but quick. Durango laughed coldly as he held the gun ready, aimed loosely at Kenny, just sort of waggling impatiently while looking at his watch. "Thirty seconds." He got serious now, starting to aim, holding the gun with both hands in a military stance.

A popping noise.

Durango's eyes rolled up. A dark spot appeared in his forehead. He collapsed and disappeared behind his car. Kenny dove for cover on the passenger side. He fumbled to get his gun out.

A whining sound approached rapidly. Afraid of a bomb, Kenny cowered on the ground with his arms wrapped around his head. He dropped his gun on the icy asphalt. He was so low that he could see under the car. There lay Durango, crumpled up, with blood oozing from the hole atop his expressionless face, like a third eye, and one hand limply thrown back with his gun inches away from his dead fingers.

The whining sound turned into a buzzing noise. It grew louder and now Kenny could see what it was. The unmanned drone that had killed Durango rolled to a stop on the road, inches from the corpse's feet.

12. The Postman Rings Again

The car had turned its headlights back on, speeded up, and now screeched to a halt right behind the black car.

"Kenny!" yelled the unmistakable voice of George Beasley. "Relax! I'm on your side."

Kenny rose and put his gun away. If Beasley were lying, there was nothing to be done about it. The same instinct that had led him to mistrust Durango now had him trust Beasley more than he had before. Kenny said: "What the hell is going on here?"

Beasley laughed happily as he came and grasped Kenny's hands to shake them. "You don't know how lucky you are."

"Oh, yes I do."

"That medallion I gave you. I'm the Postmaster for this sector of the Temporale. I'm POSENT, not this swine from TRANSENT. So when you squeezed the medallion and alerted me, I knew the game was on. Harrison and his brother were going to defect, and this idiot was going to drive them."

"What do you mean?" It had all gone so smoothly. What could be wrong with that?

"He's an idiot. Was, I should say. Part Two begins, but not what he thought. Come on into the car, where you can get warm. We are heading back to California."

Kenny stood his ground. Legs apart, he waved his arms and pointed toward Canada. "I want to go there, not there." He pointed south into America. "This is bullshit."

"I know," Beasley said patiently. "We want to make it just little less bullshit. I need your help. I promise you won't be harmed, at least not by POSENT. Look inside yourself. I know you don't know about your contract, but you will be glad you stuck by the bargain." He put the drone in the trunk of his car.

Kenny understood that, deep down, without knowing exactly why. He reached into Durango's pocket and extracted both the wallet and the envelope. A quick count told him he now had over two thousand dollars. Durango's share had been five times his own.

He got in, and Beasley started for California. "Want some coffee?"

"I could use something," Kenny said. "I'm glad to be alive."

"That was no fun back there," Beasley said agreeingly, and offered a thermos.

Kenny accepted it. The top served as a cup. The joe was black, bitter, hot, and bracing. Like life itself, it tasted wonderful just now. "What about him back there? What happens when all those paranoid cops and soldiers find him?"

"The bullet that killed him was the exact equivalent of a French Dassault-Retorne sniper rifle bullet. These people have such a rabid and unnatural hatred of the French—whom none of them have ever met, since they hide behind their Maginot Line here—that they'll think some evil French commies have invaded the area and killed the general's driver. It gets better. They'll think the general and his brother the trillionaire were on their patriotic way back to the fatherland, and were kidnapped by French terrorists. They'll be busy scouring every inch of ice and snow for miles around looking for signs of cheese and red wine and brioches that we'll be clean gone by the time they give up."

"That's pretty funny."

"Yeah, except it's not going to quite play out that way. You see, Harrison and his brother aren't just defecting. They're going to announce it to the world, and claim they are going to ally themselves with the Government of West Canada, but their real goal is to start infiltrating West Canada and take it over in addition to their huge holdings in America. I'm pretty sure Harrison's goal is to unseat the dear leader and make himself the Great Shepherd. No amount of power is enough for people like this, and they can never stop scheming."

Kenny said: "So is the whole world like that wonderful place I was just in?"

Beasley laughed. "Yes, of course. While these ultra-paranoid nuts shiver in the shelter of their Dear Leader, the Great Shepherd—to distinguish him from his immediate boss, the Good Shepherd up in heaven—the rest of the world has a thriving global economy, healthcare for everyone, low taxes, an incredible industrial boom. And they're not destroying the environment like the corporations and their media mouthpieces here. It's green, like that dome city you saw in Torquay. Funny thing. For years, Torquay was just an intersection in the middle of nowhere. They became wealthy from America's lying, apparatchik elite wining and dining and shopping across the border. While they paint monster pictures about the horrors of Canada and Europe, they freely cross back and forth. You know what? Rumors do get out. We have allies..."

"We?"

"POSENT, ever gently tweaking the past in oh-so-tiny ways, working with resistance groups. There are still a lot of good, kind people here in the military industrial corpocracy. Give people true information, don't intimidate legislators, don't buy and sell judges, and there is some faint hope they may join the rest of the world. It's happened before. Unified and prosperous Korea is just one example. The north had a Dear Leader once too."

Kenny didn't know what Korea was, but it sounded pretty big. He once again enjoyed the vast meta-highway and its dreamy flow of lights. Damn, it's good to still be alive, he thought over and over again. He could still see into the barrel of Durango's pistol. "I have some strange looking scars," Kenny said. "I must have been a soldier somewhere, huh?"

"You were a policeman, and a very brave one. We were glad to get you to work for us."

"Am I going to have my memories back? I feel like a retard."

"You'll have it all back, what there still is."

"Was my wife murdered?"

"Oh my God."

"You left the bus pass for me, didn't you?"

"Yes. I was trying to stimulate a little neural freedom in your head to loosen you a bit from the grip of TRANSENT. I didn't mean for you to remember that much."

"Who recruited me?"

"POSENT. Top level. But the mission was subverted along the way. Someone in the bureaucracy had a pet theory that TRANSENT would handle it better. TRANSENT didn't know I was already here, working on another mission. I got wind of Durango's rogue operation and put my scarce resources to work. He never knew I was watching him. He also didn't know that the Harrisons are a couple of vipers, planning something very different."

"I can believe anything."

"Yeah, see, what's happening is that Harrison is a megalomaniac who wants to not only own America. He wants to make the entire world a swamp of lies and fear like he's made of his own homeland. Canada split into three countries years ago. He wants to take over West Canada, which is highly industrialized, using the same tactics they used on the former United States. Buy the media. Spread rumors. Instill fear. Destroy social security because it's socialist. Deny healthcare because it's communism. Bring misery because it strengthens the spine. Steal the tax money to wage illegal and worthless wars that make the rich richer and fill the hospitals with maimed troops. Privatize the entire country so it's one big business octopus with tentacles everywhere, leaching away profits for the elite. It's an old pattern that's always worked in human societies. Tell the sheep they must be terrified lest Big Government take over—which is already owned by the corporations. Focus people's fear and misery on outsiders, on supposed enemies within. Create hate groups and hated groups— usually powerless minorities, and thinking people who see through the sham. It works beautifully each time. Controlling the world's only superpower, they have the military clout to be a terrible threat to the world.."

"And we're going to stop them?" Kenny almost laughed.

"We have a weapon," Beasley said. "Harrison's daughter Cheryl. You know, that beautiful blonde Olympic athlete? She is a member of the secret resistance. Nobody else in Harrison's family has any idea—yet. My mission, and I need you along, is to do what Durango just did. Bring her safely through 1,500 miles of hostile, dangerous territory, in the heart of the beast, and get her into Western Canada, where she can testify before Parliament, and destroy the plans of her father and his elite faction. "

Kenny said: "So, as you say, Harrison wants to be the next Great Shepherd."

"Exactly," Beasley said. "You're picking things up quickly." He continued: "There are also several hundred billionaires in America. Those are the dukes and barons and counts, the archdukes, the grand dukes, the viziers, what have you. It's the same old crap, just with new names and different sorts of funny hats. They govern through a quasi-religious belief system fed by their pet media and by their pawn legislators pretending to conduct democracy. West Canada still has checks and balances, law and order, halfway independent media. Harrison seems to think it's a big, ripe fruit just waiting to be plucked. Cheryl Harrison will be a better weapon than all the bombs on earth."

"How big is this resistance?"

"Hard to say. Still pretty weak. Some of the troops and police serving on the Wall near Torquay have seen the dukes come and go. They've seen the expensive fur coats, the jewelry, the liquor, the perfume. Even in a prison state like this, it's impossible to keep the truth hidden forever. At least a small number of people have the brains and the courage and the ethics to think for themselves."

"Okay, I'm in."

"There is no time to waste. My people are getting Cheryl ready in a secret safe house."

"Your people—like that old man in the library?"

"You're on to that. You're not retarded at all."

"Give me back my complete brain."

"Not yet. It would be too painful for you, and would compromise the mission. Just wait. It's for the best. You'll have to deal with the truth when that time comes." He gave Kenny a sad look. "Yes, your wife. I'm sorry. She's gone and we can't bring her back."

"Why? Is it a tweak or a change? Would it hurt the City?"

"That's not for us to decide in the field. The CloudMasters run galaxies of data and make very complex decisions. On Carly, it's no."

"Carly… Did she and I live in Talmadge?"

"Whizzago," Beasley said sharply, giving Kenny a piercing look. He snapped his finger loudly. "Be still. Forget. Feel good."

Carly. The name meant something, and yet didn't. He couldn't put his finger on it. *Talmadge.*

Tears.

13. Under The Grid (Resist)

Kenny sat back with his coffee and enjoyed the dreamy scenery high up under the stars. He was so glad to be alive. As dawn arose, the car left the mega-highway and came to ground near El Centro.

Beasley drove toward San Diego—through the desert, on the old Interstate 8, still going 100 miles an hour. There were no speed limits in the land of the free. Police patrols were visible at regular intervals, but they weren't looking for speeders. The desert shimmered in winter sunlight, its rolling sandy hillocks dotted with cactus and scrub. In winter, it could be hot but not unbearable, with chops of tropical cumulus cloud from the Mexican jungles low on the horizon, full of rain, stacked against each other like woolly bags on a warehouse dock.

At intervals, to the south across the flat landscape, you could see the distant gray-black ribbon of the Great American National Border Wall—here, arrayed against Mexico.

Then came the mountains—a barrier keeping the desert sky contained, a harbor sheltering galleons of puffy clouds. Dark granitic mountain masses loomed a mile high, covered in heavy green foliage that belonged more to the Rocky Mountains than to the arid coast of Southern California. Beasley and Kenny engaged in little conversation as the last hours of their trek unwound.

"It's not going to be as easy getting her into Canada," Beasley said." I can't risk trying a repeat of the Harrisons, and in any case their car is gone. By now, the cops will be all over that."

Kenny suddenly remembered the tour book. "I have some old maps."

"Did the librarian set you up?"

"Yes. He took away the book I wanted to read, and gave me an old tour book."

"We'll have to cruise by your place and pick it up." Beasley drove down long grade toward the coast, coming into sandy, low land. The air here was stuffier and richer. There were abrupt round hills, covered with huge sandstone boulders, whose tips had once been islands in a shallow peninsular sea populated with dinosaurs and their contemporaries.

"Where are the ruined houses with crazy people living in them?" Kenny asked. He remembered the woman with the cleaver.

"Not sure," Beasley said. "When we planted you here, we had to be careful not to make the insertion point obvious. Don't forget, nobody in this world knows people like me exist. Nobody knows anything about the Temporale. We salvage people's memories., kind of a meme soup, for missions like this. We spliced someone's memories into yours to cover you from yourself, and from any possible police scan. The authorities here are starting to develop some primitive methods to pick up people's thought waves."

"So these are the memories of a dead person?"

Beasley nodded. "Someone who was murdered in one of those dead-end streets back in Albany. A young man and his sister, who were innocently taking a walk one Sunday afternoon. You've never been to Albany, at least not in this time period. Don't worry—those memories will fade."

Kenny tested his memory and sure enough, the violent, jerky film of the crazy woman running after the girl with a cleaver was becoming hazy. Good. He wanted to purge himself of that vision. There was enough terror in his life as it was.

Beasley drove down El Cajon Boulevard and south into Golden Hills. A smell of smoke hung in the air as they drew near Kenny's neighborhood. The library had burned down. There were bodies lined up in gray nylon bags on the sidewalk. Police and Fire Department vehicles sat parked at odd angles all around. The street was covered with a criss-cross of thick hoses, and partially flooded. Outside the yellow plastic secure zone, crowds stood thickly with folded arms, watching, brooding, solemn-faced.

"I need that book," Beasley said, driving past.

"Maybe the old man knew they were going to get hit," Kenny said. "Maybe he gave me the book for safe keeping."

Beasley kept looking back over his shoulder at the disaster. "I dunno. I dunno. I dunno. Well, we have to do something. I'll stop here." He pulled up under a large tree a little way down the street from Kenny's walkup. "You feel brave? Got your permit in case anyone stops you?"

Kenny nodded.

"We'll play it safe." Beasley gave him some instructions on where to meet him.

Kenny got out, and Beasley drove away. Acting casually, Kenny crossed the street and headed for his building. He clomped up the stairs, unlocked his room, and stepped inside. He looked carefully around in the silent gloom. It looked as if nothing had been touched. The window was half open as he'd left it, with the plastic curtain draped up over the rod. In the window, hanging over the ledge, were his other overalls, now dry. The collar kept stirring faintly in the wind. Over the treetops, which stirred slightly, was the women's house and the grassy yard. Not a soul in sight—they must all be at work at their women's jobs, in places men did not go during the day. Kenny poked around in his locker and saw everything was exactly as he'd left it. None of that stuff was his—the school ring, the towels, socks, the comb. It had all been planted to make him believe he had a past here. He grabbed the map from its envelope, but left the envelope in place. He stuffed the map in his overall pocket and stepped outside. He locked the door and put the key in his pocket, as if he were coming back. Which he knew he never would. It would take them a few days to figure that out.

He walked down the stairs. With each footstep, he expected a hammer to descend from behind or above. Was anyone watching? Surely by now they'd miss him at Sunday services. With Durango presumably found by now, there would be a frantic search for Harrison and his brother. Kenny stepped out the door, across the little concrete porch, and down the stairs. He turned left at the sidewalk and walked at a normal pace, feeling pressure pounding in his ears, but he kept his composure.

No sooner had he passed through the shade of a large lemon-gum eucalyptus tree, with gray bark peeling from its yellow trunk, than four police cruises came silently streaking down the street and screeched to a stop before his building. A dozen men in dark armor, waving assault rifles, ran on booted feet to surround the building. A black command post vehicle, large as a bus, with no windows or writing on it, pulled up across the street. Kenny ducked around the corner. He passed the grocery where he'd bought his evening beer. Shopkeepers, rubbing their hands in their white aprons, stepped outside to gawk at the fuss. Kenny walked down toward Florida Canyon, toward Balboa Park, with the city skyline in the distance before him. He had a good thirty minute hike, down into Florida Canyon via grassy meadows that had once been a golf course, across crumbling Pershing Drive, through the ruins of the old naval hospital, and up onto Park Boulevard.

Near the San Diego Zoo, he waited at the bus stop on Park Boulevard. Around him swirled flocks of school children being taken to see the animals. There were still elephants, giraffes, and lions, as well as pythons and alligators, though many of the more exotic animals were extinct. None of the adults looked like detectives. Kenny relaxed. When the bus came wheezing and laboring along, he got on board and paid from his blue wallet. He sat in the rear, where he could keep an eye on everyone. There weren't many people on the bus. One man with sunglasses looked his way, and Kenny looked out the window. An old lady sat with a large handbag on her lap. People got on, people got off, but nobody seemed suspicious. This was critical. If one cop spotted him, if they even knew to look for him, every cop in the city would know within a minute. They were all connected on a cell grid, something that had been available to the general population during the Good Old Days, but now was a tool restricted to the government.

In Mission Valley, Kenny transferred to a red trolley. He rode, whizzing at 100 feet above rooftops and river reeds, toward downtown San Diego. Downtown, at the Santa Fe Terminal by the harbor, he got out and made his way east by northeast into the warren of buildings around C street. He kept watching glass windows around him for reflections of anyone following him, but saw nobody—there were only leaves rustling in the wind, blue sky, women in nice clothes rushing to their office jobs. He started breathing easier. No sign of any floating eyes or hovering drones, either. With luck, he was still below the grid. He'd been expecting to hear sirens, to see more police cars, but Tom Rogers' Daily Chat had not broken the story yet. Maybe they wouldn't. Maybe they'd hush it up, as the outside world might expect this closed kingdom of paranoia to behave. The rulers would not want their serfs to know that a high duke had defected—that might imply there was something other than radioactive swamps and socialist monsters outside the Wall. The Harrisons' gambit was aimed at fooling the leaders of West Canada into complacency.

On an obscure block around B and Grape Streets, he was walking in the shade of an old glassy building, when he heard a brief toot. Beasley pulled up alongside him, and Kenny got into the front passenger seat. "Got the book?"

Kenny nodded and held it up.

"Good—start looking at the smaller roads up near the border. There is an underground drainage system about a hundred miles east of Torquay. Goes right under the wall. My contacts in the underground tell me they can get us through, but the trick will be reaching them. Once we're within the last ten miles of the wall, a guide will see us across. Someone who was in the Border army, saw what's really going on, and joined the resistance."

Kenny became aware of rustling sounds behind him, and turned. There sat a young woman, with a still younger man and woman. "Hello," Kenny said, and they nodded to him. He recognized them from the videos and pictures. They were nice looking young people—the blonde, Cheryl, wearing a conservative business suit with pleated tartan skirt and a gray jacket over crisp white blouse; the young man, a cousin named Phillip, a dark brown wool turtleneck sweater with muted blue and burgundy accents knitted in, and gray slacks; the younger woman, Melody, wearing a pink dress with frilly white sleeves and a white belt with matching white leather purse and shoes. All three wore sturdy shoes for hiking.

As he looked more closely, he saw that Melody had the dark, delicate beauty of her mother. She had long black hair and huge dark eyes full of emotion and feeling. It was said of her that she was the pious one in the family, the one most likely to succeed her aunt as director of American Christian Charities. Cheryl, Kenny knew, had cousins who were robust and blond or red-headed like her. They rode horses, played polo, were ambitious and competitive and always seemed to win. They worked hard, competed hard, played hard, loved hard, and in a way they were the explanation of how Trent Harrison's grandfather and father had risen from humble origins to control a significant piece of America.

Cheryl Harrison leaned forward and put her hand on Kenny's wrist. "I understand you are the brave man who will help us get to the other side. Thank you." She was an attractive woman in that she had a fresh, scrubbed, athletic look. Her blonde hair was cut short. She said: "I'm bringing my sister Melody along, and our cousin Phillip Harrison."

"Sure," Kenny said, "we'll do all we can to make sure you're safe."

Melody, sitting by the window opposite Cheryl, glowered. She was really a dark-haired, pale young woman, just like in the pictures. She twisted her hands awkwardly in her lap and looked near tears. Phillip was a quiet, gallant young man with a blond buzz cut. He looked a bit like Cheryl, but thinner. He didn't have her athletic boldness and determination. You could see that right way, Kenny thought. Phillip patted Melody's hands reassuringly. He was a princely looking young man, Kenny thought, in a delicate sort of way. Melody impulsively thrust her right arm under Phillip's left arm, and pressed her face against his shoulder. She looked fearful and jumpy.

"Everything's going to all right, Ma'am," Kenny assured Melody. "I promise you."

"I agree," Beasley said heartily as he swung the car onto Interstate 8 for the ride east to the great mega-superhighway that would take them to Canada in a few hours, traveling at great cruising speeds.

An emotional debate began, which would rise between hysterical tears and silent time spans, to continue all the way to the Canadian border. This journey, unlike the other two, was not a pleasant one for Kenny. He didn't have time to savor the lights on the great road, the stars above, the flying cars with red taillights on this side, with white headlights going the other way on the opposite span.

"Honey," Cheryl said to her sister, "you can believe these two wonderful men. We're going to be really free in a few hours, for the first time in our lives." To Kenny she said: "She's never been outside. She's pretty delicate. She was sent away to religious school, and believes all the propaganda."

"I've been to Canada, Ma'am," Kenny said to Cheryl. "I agree. I understand what you mean."

Melody, however, gasped and stared at Kenny with unbelieving eyes. Her look was one of horror. "Oh no. These are Canadian or European agents. We're being kidnapped." She burst into tears and flailed her arms wildly as she cried: "I told you, Cheryl, you're a fool. These men are going to hold us for ransom over in that communist hell hole. I want to go back home!"

As Melody tried to unlock her door with scratching, clawing fingers, Beasley yelled: "Hey! You're going to fall out. Come on, Melody, I'm driving over 400 miles an hour. Nobody's going to hurt you."

Phillip manfully climbed over Melody and sat by the door to block her. Cheryl embraced her terrified sister and hugged her in a powerful grip. "We're going to meet mommy and daddy on the other side in a few hours."

"It's a lie!" Melody cried. "You're lying. Why would mommy and daddy go over to our enemies?"

"You have to trust me," Cheryl said firmly. "You'll understand everything when daddy explains it to you."

Kenny regarded Beasley in shock. So Beasley had not told Melody and Phillip the truth. Cheryl had apparently had to lie to get her sister even this far.

Melody sobbed heart-brokenly into a handkerchief she took from her purse. Phillip and Cheryl hugged and comforted her. Phillip told Melody: "I don't really believe them either, cousin, but Cheryl is the leader. We have to do what she says."

Melody was silent for a while. Then she looked hysterically at Cheryl and shrieked through her tears: "I can't believe how you are betraying us and your country!"

"Easy," Phillip said, pulling her toward himself.

Cheryl spoke firmly: "Listen, Melody. That cuts both ways. You might start yelling when we crawl past the border guards on the American side, and get us all killed."

"Better dead than red," Melody said, reciting an old slogan.

"I'd rather stay alive," Phillip muttered thickly, looking aside resentfully.

"We have to make a deal," Cheryl said. "You go along with us, and keep quiet. When we get to the border, you can look for yourself. If you don't like what you see, you can turn back."

Melody thought about this. Her reply, however, came from a different angle. "If you are right, then our parents have betrayed everything we believe in. Our whole lives."

"Why don't you hold off your judgments and let mommy and daddy explain their side of the story?"

Melody glowered at her.

Phillip muttered: "Come on, cousin, loosen up. Maybe Cheryl has a point."

"I can't," Melody said haltingly. "I'm terrified."

Cheryl said: "Everything you've been told is a lie. There is no freedom here. It's a corporate police state run on lies and terror."

"Impossible," Melody said. She kneaded her handkerchief in both agitated fists.

"Will you give me a chance?" Cheryl pleaded. "I'm your sister. I love you. I would not lead you astray."

"What if I believe you?" Melody said with haunted eyes. "Maybe you're telling the truth. But it's all so complicated. It's just easier to think that the devil has taken possession of you. The socialists have brainwashed you."

Phillip said: "Come on, cousin. That's a bit much." Kenny thought Phillip looked torn between the two women. There was his older cousin Cheryl, whom he loved and admired. She was always the leader. Then there was his cousin Melody, closer to him in age and character—inward, quiet, thoughtful—and Melody's argument fell to the side of what they'd always been told. They evidently were not privy to the darkest secret of the elite—that they regularly visited, and shopped in, the outside world that was supposedly a howling wilderness of demons, a veritable antechamber of hell.

Cheryl shook her head sorrowfully. "You poor kid, to believe all that. We are the super-rich. When you're one of us, and you reach the right age, mommy and daddy tell you the truth and take you shopping. You'll see how great life really is over there. The common people actually have complete universal healthcare, which our brainwashed people have been told is evil communism. The West Canadians are safe and secure. Nobody works seventy hours a week in a dirty factory and goes home to eat rancid food. Yes, you haven't experienced our wonderful world of the Great Shepherd's America, have you? You've been sheltered and well-fed in your private schools..."

Melody started crying again, this time more gently. "...I do care about average people."

Cheryl put aside her annoyance after a moment and ran her arm around Melody's shoulders, hugging her to her. "Honey, I know you do. It's all just a big shock, isn't it?'

"Tell us the truth," Phillip said. "Is it really true that your mom and dad have defected to West Canada?"

There was a silence in the car. Beasley made a sharp intake of breath. Kenny worried that this added factor was going to totally make Melody break down. He glanced at the dashboard and saw that they'd traveled past the halfway point. They were over Wyoming now, and would soon start descending into Montana.

"It's true," Cheryl said, "but they aren't traitors. It's a secret plot to take over West Canada and make it part of America. They want to take over the whole world."

Phillip looked at Cheryl, disgusted, as if he'd just discovered she were a murderer. "And you want to stop them?"

Now the truth is out, Kenny thought.

Melody held her hands to her ears and looked as if she were about to scream. For a full three or four minutes, there was a tense silence in the car. Cheryl pulled Melody's right hand from the right ear and laid it in her lap. Phillip looked blankly away, out the window, as if he were saturated and could take no more. Cheryl said, "Listen, sister, you have to trust me. Everything will turn out just right for all of us. We are doing the right thing. America will be better off, we'll be better off, you'll be happy you did the right thing—and like I said, when you get your first look at the real outside world, you'll see I'm right."

Kenny couldn't resist adding: "She's right, Ma'am. I've seen it. It's a beautiful, peaceful, shiny place full of lights and happy people. You will love it!"

For the rest of the way, the three Harrisons in the back remained quiet. They sat quietly, looking left and right at the passage of lights and trucks and bridge pylons in the night.

Kenny studied the tour book and penciled in the most likely route to get to the ten mile zone.

Beasley started the descent into Montana. They all had coffee and donuts from a thermal cooler. The car started down a long exit ramp that put it on the Interstate system and then, soon enough, onto the same frozen wilderness roads where Kenny had seen

Durango shot. He wondered idly if Beasley still had the drone in the trunk.

On one or two occasions, shadowy figures stood by the roadside. "Who are those people?" Melody whispered.

"Those are the orphans American Christian Charities supposedly rescues from the cities," Cheryl said. "They bring them up here, work them to death, but some lose their minds and are of no further use, so they're allowed out. They just wander around looking for anything they can eat, until they starve or freeze to death. But they've learned all the right Bible verses. That's something you can go back and change for the better, Melody. That's why you need to help us escape, so we can make our sick country better again."

Phillip sobbed quietly. Melody seemed expressionless, veiled in shadows.

They drove for a long time on smaller country roads. In the distant north were the lights of the Great American Border Wall. Wisps of steam rose from factory chimneys. Patrolling aircraft with winking red lights flew search patterns. "They are probably still in an uproar over Durango," Kenny suggested.

"I don't doubt it," Beasley said, "but that's a hundred miles west of here." He pulled to a halt off the road among a grove of snowy trees. "Here we are." He held up the key. "Nobody is going back. But I'll tell you what. When we reach the border"—he spoke directly to Melody and Phillip—"I'm going to offer you this key if you decide to go back. And now the unfortunate part." He held up his automatic. "If anyone tries to signal to the border troops or betray us in any way, I will kill that person without hesitation. This mission is too important, and good people have died to get us here, so I don't want any one full of stupid ideas to try and betray us. I'm sorry, but that needs to be clear. Do you all understand?"

One by one, Cheryl, Phillip, and then Melody nodded. Melody hung her head sadly.

"Everything is going to be all right," Cheryl whispered to her sister.

* * * *

"There we go," said Beasley energetically, shoving his door open. Two hooded figures approached. "Those are resistance members. Don't ask them any questions and they won't ask you anything. That way, anyone gets captured, they won't give anything away under torture. Oh yes, the Army of the Borders tortures people to make them talk." He pointed to a pile of coats in the far back of the car. "Put those on. It's colder than Hades out here." Kenny also donned his olive green, nylon web gear with gun and ammo clips.

Beasley trudged across the snow and conferred briefly with the young man and woman who had come to guide them the last few miles to the Milk River tributary that ran under the Wall.

Kenny stood with Cheryl, while Phillip hovered protectively around Melody. Cheryl impulsively rushed to hug her sister, who looked distraught. "You'll be brave, darling, won't you?" Cheryl asked Melody.

For the first time, Melody smiled through her tears. She wiped her eyes with her handkerchief and nodded uncertainly. "Yes. I will."

"Good girl," Cheryl enthused. "I promise you, everything will be so much better by this evening. We'll join mommy and daddy at a nice steak house. I'll buy you a nice Canadian beer. How's that! Everyone is so friendly!"

"Let's go," Beasley urged. "We're going to cross some fields, and then go through a forest. That will put us halfway to the wall. When we come out of the forest we will cross through some mine fields and reach a river. There is a dam near the river, holding a large lake that's a reservoir used by people on both sides of the border. We're practically safe and clear at that point, because we go into the concrete redoubts on the other side of the dam, down through the tunnels, and into the secret drainage channels that cross under the wall. Melody, your mom and dad will be there to meet us on the Canadian side when we step out. You'll see. "

Cheryl rubbed Melody's shoulder for reassurance. Melody bravely linked arms with Phillip and they all started walking on the crunchy snow.

The two guides were already hiking away toward the north. They remained shadowy figures in their dark clothing. Large hoods veiled their pale faces, and Kenny would never get a good look at them. He felt a twinge of fear himself. What if Beasley was being betrayed by EXENT or TRANSENT, or even by his own people in POSENT? What if they were being led into a trap? What if Harrison's trillionaire enemies wanted to kidnap his children? Too many angles, too many possibilities. All Kenny could do was trudge along.

The walk seemed endless. Even in bulky, warm clothing, the bitter cold penetrated and went for your spine.

The guides knew their ground and walked steadily. The pace was fast—the sooner they reached the Wall, the better. At times one or the other of those following them stumbled. They were all wet and cold from falling into snow banks and puddles by the time the Wall loomed overhead.

Melody at first recoiled from the black, steel-studded fortress wall. Perhaps the sight of so many American flags made her eyes look teary, her features determined. She clung to Phillip, or was it Phillip clinging to her? Kenny brought up the rear, as was his duty. Both he and Beasley were the armed soldiers here. The resistance members stayed far ahead, and would be able to melt away to fight again another day, should the mission fail.

Cheryl walked up ahead with Beasley. He and she were equally sturdy, determined, sure of themselves.

Phillip and Melody walked ten or fifteen feet behind them, and Kenny another twenty feet behind them, too far to hear more than the murmur of their conversation. More and more, it appeared that Phillip was losing his nerve, and Melody was encouraging him. He appeared to grow more frightened. She seemed to grow stronger. Maybe it was starting to really sink in for Phillip. He was about to violate every fiber of his being, every ounce of brainwashing that had saturated him with those false pieties for his entire life. By contrast, Melody appeared to be becoming more assured and courageous. The tears were no more. Her face, as Kenny could see in profile from behind, in the starlight, looked vigorous and flushed from the cold. She hugged his right arm to her, pressed against him, waved her mittened right hand chattered incessantly. At one point, he stopped and stamped his foot, but she pulled on him and nodded amid a cascade of words to browbeat, to convince, to plead with him, to directly order him. Then he shrugged and went along with brisk step. She got a happy bounce in her step.

What were those two plotting, Kenny wondered with hopeful puzzlement. They were like the rest of the population who must be brought over, he thought. The veil of lies and fear had to be penetrated, blown away, torn away by sunlight and truth. If Melody could do it, she could lead others to the truth.

A helicopter with flashing red lights approached thunderously. Those on the run threw themselves face-down and lay still. Their guides disappeared. Kenny experienced another moment of terror. A circle of light speeded along the ground ahead of the chopper. It thundered overhead and vanished into a silence above some dense forest nearby. Like phantoms, the guides reappeared and kept walking. They went into the forest itself. There they stopped and uncoiled a twenty-foot rope. "Hold on to this and don't let go," Beasley whispered. "They are going to lead us past the listening devices and traps. There are places where it's a hundred foot drop into a river full of mean-looking boulders, so be careful. Stick together. We'll spread out later."

Kenny made a loop of the end of the rope and put his hand in it. The gun weighed heavily at his right side, the ammo clips on his left. There were moments when he heard a slight sob or a sigh from Phillip or Melody. Kenny heard Melody whisper to Phillip: "Be brave, cousin."

At times, he heard river water pounding among wet boulders far below. It was so pitch-dark that he couldn't see the river, just a flash of white water at odd moments in tree clearings. He could smell water vapor. At one point, Phillip slipped on wet clay and fell to his knees. Kenny rescued him from a bad fall by grabbing him from behind, while Melody grabbed him from the front.

At last, they came out of the woods. Several rows of rusty concertina wire ran east and west as far as they could see. Beasley whispered: "The mine field." The guides lifted the wire with poles so the others could pass underneath.

The guides, carrying their poles, led them carefully through the death field. They all clung together on the rope. After a few hundred feet, they reached another stretch of concertina wire— they had made it safely through. Again, the guides lifted the wire.

Once the group were on the other side, the guides left the poles for some other party, and headed north.

The view here was breathtaking. For just a moment, the party halted atop a ridge, with the forest behind them and winding on to their right.

The Wall loomed as high as a ten story building, higher than the ridge on which Kenny and his companions stood. The Wall's dark, streaked surfaces were studded with sensors, lights, and alarms. The row of flags fluttered overhead in a slight breeze. In the valley below, amid a massive cover of trees, ran a few barely hidden military roads. Here and there stood concrete sheds. That was far below, and of course there was no gate here, so this was a blind spot.

The guides did not slacken their pace. With a steep drop on their left, and the dense forest on their right, they walked along a wide path. They didn't need the rope any longer, so Beasley had wound it up and hung it across his shoulders.

Beyond a bend ahead was a high dam, almost as high as the Wall. The dam was almost entirely visible except for the forest projecting a corner out along a bend in the path.

Beyond that overhang of trees, the dam's striated, curving face rose up from the rushing river below. It glowed in starlight. Beyond the dam were blockhouses hidden in thick forestation that ran right up to the dam on one side, and touched the Wall a few hundred feet beyond. It looked closer than that. The immensity of the Wall, and the immensity of the dam, and the huge valley to his left, made Kenny get a vertiginous sense of disproportion, almost a dizziness and a ringing in his ears. These huge structures had a toy-like quality.

Kenny followed the others around the bend and onto a concrete apron. They walked indistinctly ahead of him in single file. A concrete path about ten feet wide led some 400 feet across the top of the dam to another concrete apron on the other side. They were close to freedom now. As Beasley had said, once they crossed the dam, they'd enter the tunnels and be home free. Kenny thought back with great joy to the bright lights and clean streets of Torquay, and knew he'd soon be having a beer and a nice steak dinner. And he'd be wearing some nice clothing instead of these stinking overalls. Feeling the wind buffeting him, he clung to the steel railing on one side of the path and made it across the bridge in a few minutes. On the opposite apron stood the guides, Cheryl, and Beasley.

Cheryl came at Kenny, her eyes radiating horror. "Where are they?"

"What?" Kenny saw her look and got a sick feeling.

He turned and looked at the great dam, with its gleaming plunge nearly ten stories.

"No!" Cheryl screamed and started to run back across the dam.

But it was too late. Melody and Phillip had hidden, then followed behind Kenny, and now stood together on the middle of the dam. They looked tiny, the two, holding each other.

Kenny felt a sort of frozen, grotesque disbelief as he watched the two shadowy figures.

Phillip stepped hesitantly to the edge in the middle of the dam.

"No!" Cheryl screamed. "No," Kenny and Beasley yelled simultaneously.

Melody spoke encouragingly to her cousin and patted his chest lovingly.

They nodded to each other, held hands, and jumped.

Beasley cursed behind Kenny.

Cheryl stopped running and stood holding onto the railing.

The two bodies still held hands as they tumbled through the air.

They were dark dots, each with a pair of legs stiffly extended as if standing. Their faces were tiny pale dots. They held hands to the last. It seemed a long way down from where Kenny stood.

They came apart about halfway down when they hit the curving concrete.

Now they were two separate, bouncing bundles of flesh and clothing.

The bodies bounced like rag dolls each time they hit.

They struck repeatedly on the curving stone until they disappeared into the tree crowns below.

Cheryl held her hands to her mouth, doubled over, and emitted a long-drawn, hoarse wail that rose and fell in bereavement.

Kenny felt terrible. He knew he had failed, just when victory seemed within reach.

Beasley cursed again. Then he seemed to realize Kenny's sense of loss. "You could not have seen that coming. None of us did. I'm the leader. I take responsibility."

Cheryl ran up and pummeled Kenny's chest with her fists, so he fell back. "I'm sorry," he said.

She ran to Beasley and started hitting him. "You two were supposed to protect us. To take care of us. I just lost my sister and my cousin!" Then she crumpled to the ground and cried heartbrokenly.

Beasley and Kenny walked to the middle of the dam and looked down. Kenny saw two broken things on the glowing concrete far below. Black ooze was spreading below the two objects. "I could rappel down and get them," Beasley said to Kenny. "They're gone and we don't have time." He glanced toward Cheryl. "I'll get her into Canada if I have to force her at gun point."

"I feel terrible," Kenny said.

"Me too," Beasley said.

They walked back to the woman, who still lay brokenly crying and hitting the ground with her hands. "Ma'am," Beasley said, leaning over her.

She screamed and rose to claw at him.

Beasley restrained her. "Stop. Stop. Stop."

She slumped a bit, pushed him away, and stood with her arms folded and her head hanging.

One of the guides, the woman, stepped out of the woods while the man remained in the shadows. "We'll climb down and get them. We need to hide the bodies, actually. We'll give them a decent burial, and you can reclaim them when you want, to take them home."

The woman said to Cheryl: "Please don't fail in your mission, Cheryl. We need you so badly to succeed and stop your father. " With one last, soulful look, the woman turned and she and her companion vanished into the woods.

Beasley told Cheryl: "Ma'am, he and I failed in an important part of our mission. There is nothing we can say that will bring your loved ones back. I'm sorry. Let's get moving."

Kenny stepped forward, hoping he wouldn't get too rough with her. "I'm sorry too. What you have to do now is get to the mission that this is all about. If you lose your way now, then your sister and cousin really died in vain, for nothing."

She sniffled and looked at him, eyes filled with tears. She nodded. After a long, awkward, pregnant silence, she whispered: "Let's go."

From there, it was a miserable, cold climb ever downward, through brick cisterns and concrete barrel vaults, past pillars of steel and over steel-wire walkways, lit faintly by mesh-covered industrial bulbs. When they reached valley ground level, the path took them into raw granite under the Great Wall. Beasley flicked on a small flashlight that guided them. The flood channel sloped down, until they reached a slippery concrete trough. A shallow stream of icy, foaming water flowed past them. It was just wide enough for Kenny to get across in one massive leap. Beasley followed. Cheryl leaped on powerful legs, but slipped, and wound up in the cold water. Weak and sobbing, she splashed through the water and emerged, bawling—not about the cold, Kenny was sure, but about her terrible losses. Kenny felt like bawling, too. Somehow, deep down, he knew what it was like.

They trudged another few hundred feet upward and emerged in Canada in a clear, icy night. This side looked just like the other side, with stretches of frozen whiteness interspersed with deep, dark forests. But in the distance was the glow of a shining city. A free city.

Three unmarked cars sat parked on the road as they approached. There were Royal Canadian Mounted Police men and women in heavy winter uniform parkas, with side arms, and other people in plain clothing. In the middle stood Trent Harrison and his beautiful wife. They were impeccably and warmly dressed, and both looked grimly angry.

Cheryl stood about twenty feet away, confronting them.

When he saw the tears on Cheryl's face, and the grief in her eyes, Trent's studied arrogance broke. He began to look dismayed. His wife looked distraught, and started to go to Cheryl, but two policewomen stopped her.

"Where is Melody?" Trent demanded.

"She's dead," Cheryl wailed, "because of you!"

Her mother broke into a scream, dropping her purse and holding her hands to her mouth.

"Why did you do this?" Trent asked dully.

Beasley took Kenny by the arm. "Come on, we're done. Let's get out of here."

As Kenny walked in the direction Beasley was shoving him, a uniformed sergeant hollered: "Hey, who are those people?"

Someone said: "Guides. Leave them be." The West Canadians knew the score, and would cover for anyone working against Harrison and the Great Shepherd.

Kenny looked back, but Beasley kept pushing. "Let's get the hell out of here. Let's go."

He led Kenny toward a grove of trees at the edge of the great forest. Kenny looked back at the people who all seemed to stay frozen as they were. "What's going to happen now?"

Beasley said: "The Harrisons will be deported back to America in a few minutes. The Canadians don't want to have any paranoid atomic bomb attacks or whatever. The Great Shepherd's propaganda media will probably avoid mentioning anything. Cheryl has already ruined the plan to seize West Canada. We made sure the Premier and the Cabinet got word Cheryl was on her way, and why. Her story will be in the Canadian news by morning. The Harrisons' defection story no longer holds water. They'll go back, along with the general and his wife, and resume life like nothing happened—except they've lost their two daughters. I wonder if bastards like the Harrisons ever have feelings or learn from their greed. Well, never mind, we've got business to attend to."

14. Temporale Retour

Kenny and Beasley stood in a clearing in the middle of nowhere, about a mile from the looming Wall. Beasley said: "First of all, your name isn't Kensington."

"You planted that name, didn't you?"

"Yeah. Before TRANSENT hijacked you, I wanted you to have a bring-back about Talmadge. I'm sorry about her, Mack.'

"Mack?"

"You are Special Agent Joe Mackinson, of the DEA, an anti-drug police agency of the United States Federal Government. Yes, before the loonies totally took over, meaning corporate patsies. I'm sending you back to the same moment that TRANSENT and POSENT had that shootout over the river where you were waiting for Leo, your partner. You don't need to worry about any of it, Mack. The drug meeting gets scrubbed and you don't catch any narco-criminals that night. But you do need to go home and see what you can salvage."

"What was her name?"

"Carly."

The air started to shimmer around them as a transient Temporale portal opened. Mack was amazed to see that, where there had been nothing but snow and trees and frigidly sighing wind, there was now a station platform overlooking a huge tunnel lit by long streaky biolume lights. Beasley took him by the elbow and guided him to the platform. "I'm going to put you on board, but I have to stay here."

"What are you going to do now?" Mack asked. He felt dazed, having just seen two young kids commit suicide, and a global plot ruined, and a family drama. He was trying to gather his thoughts about Carly, but nothing came. She was an enigma of pain at the core of his soul. He only glimpsed a vision, briefly, flashing like a strobe, of a kitchen in disarray, walls splattered with blood, a young woman sprawled brokenly in a mass of gore.

A wind started to fill the tunnel. That would be the Time Train charging closer on its tracks.

"I have to go back and do whatever the City tells me to do. Maybe I'll make another tweak. Maybe I'll prevent TRANSENT from making changes. Who knows. Maybe—"

They both thought about Melody and Phillip, but couldn't say the unspeakable.

"Is there a difference between a tweak and a change?" Kenny asked.

"Yes. A tweak is something you do to change the past, but it's so minor that it gets lost in the great big tumbling river of time. A change is something more dangerous, which could lead to the ultimate nightmare, a contradiction. Like going back and killing your grandfather, which means you wouldn't be born and therefore couldn't go back to kill him, which means he lives and you're born, so you go back to kill him…and the whole thing becomes a mad loop that grows bigger and bigger until the universe creates another copy of itself—maybe one in which you were never born, or your grandfather died somehow, and the other in which you don't go back to kill him. Something like that. The cosmos is a big, mysterious place that has ways of straightening itself out."

"Like water always finding its own level," Mack said.

"Exactly. It's a law of nature, like gravity."

As the rushing wind grew stronger and warmer, Mack saw a streak of bluish-white light approaching. As the streak drew closer, it slowed down. As it slowed, it resolved from an unreadable blur into sort of cigar tube. Then the cigar tube morphed into something with wheels and lights and bumps and protrusions that slowed down and looked pretty much like a string of railway cars.

The cars squealed to a halt on rusty looking rails.

Doors slammed open.

A distant locomotive uttered several short, steamy, high-pitched whistles. It sounded impatient, as if it had many places to go.

Beasley ushered Mack onto the nearest rather plain car, which looked like any urban subway car. He pointed to a heavy steel bank of dials set in the wall. "This is the control. I'm going to set it for just the moment when our people grabbed you from the river. You'll find your car intact. Just go home." He pointed to a plain wooden bench. "Just sit there, relax, and you'll step out in Ocotillo Wells within the hour, like nothing happened.'

Mack watched as Beasley set the mechanism telling the train where and when to take him. Beasley turned and offered his hand. "Thanks for all your help. Sorry about Phillip and Melody. That can't be undone. It wasn't your fault. No matter, you'll forget all about it. I'll have to live with it for the rest of my life, sadly, but then I'm supposed to do that."

Mack offered his hand. "It's been—." He couldn't think of an adjective, but Beasley gave his hand a brief, hearty shake.

Beasley took a few steps back, off the train. On the platform, he said: "I'm going to give you the rest of your memories back, with a little delay built in. Look at me." He raised both hands, showing his palms. "I'm going to release you now."

As Mack stared at him, Beasley made a magician-like face and said: "Whizzago!" With that, he spread his hands apart as if opening a veil.

Mack felt a wave of shock as his real memories flooded his brain, and the fake memes of some dead person with the pseudonym Kensington C. Del Sol evaporated into the imagination from which they had come. The young man near Albany, who had died trying to save his sister from a madwoman with a cleaver, could finally be completely at rest.

Mack watched Beasley walk away into a shimmering light that briefly illumined the forest before the portal closed and there was just the tiled, curving wall inside the Temporale tunnel.

Just as quickly, the train started moving. Mack sat down on a somewhat hard bench and hung on to a shining, metallic handle as the train rushed ever faster, morphing back into a cigar tube and then into a smudge of bluish-white light traveling at hyper speed through the motherverse. Mack sat with his head on palms, shaking his head. He felt nauseous. That delay of which Beasley had spoken was like a narcotic, soaking his brain in confusion. He sat back and passed out.

15. Time Town, Mon Amour

In her ornate railway car cruising through Time Town, Lady Chivet Betize, Third Postal Lord, sat by her window in the library, sipping tea and looking at the golden city she loved with all her heart. Squares and rounded rectangles of light, in rich colors like stained glass, drifted slowly across her features as the city moved around outside—traffic, pedestrians, countless giant building blocks, wonderful shops and stores.

Far off in the distance shimmered the Dissolve—the scarred and wounded edge of the city where it bled into the cosmopause, an explosion in slow motion, a mass of gnawing splinters being ground back into primeval godots.

Across from the Lady Betize sat General Tenc Hoseth, of the Postal Entity (POSENT). The same tawny light drifted slowly across his features. He held the cat named Donald on his lap. Donald purred as the general stroked him behind his ears.

Seeing a faint motion on the Dissolve, Lady Betize lifted a pair of opera glasses and looked closely. "I do believe we recovered an hour or two," she said. What was lost would not reappear, but new time and contents had just appeared. For a while, the amount of splintering was slightly less. Neon cubes rearranged themselves. Several new ones appeared in the process.

She lifted her finger to the wall beside her, and as she did so, a button appeared on the wall. She pressed it. A moment later, in rushed a young woman in a gray smock who had been standing in the hall outside. "Yes, Lady?"

"I wish to speak with the special agent in the 2100-2200 home sector right away. Make my call Hyper-Secure POSENT Crypto Immediate."

"Yes, Lady." The woman went to the old-fashioned bookcases lining the wall, opened an ornate wooden cabinet, and brought out an early Victorian telephone. It was one of Lady Chivet Betize's prized trophies from her own journeys in time as a young field agent.

The maid spoke with an operator in Time Town, who made the necessary encrypted connections through the Temporale. Then she handed the phone to Lady Betize.

"Who am I speaking with?...Oh, Mr. Beasley. Yes. It appears you have done your job, and everything went well...What's that?...Yes, COTU thanks you, and POSENT will reward you with a raise and a promotion. I think we should show our gratitude to Mr. Mackinson then, since he served so faithfully...Pardon me?"

Beasley jabbered distantly.

"His wife? No, I forbid saving her."

Beasley jabbered some more.

Chivet was firm. "I understand that Mr. Mackinson will be sad. I absolutely forbid it. Saving her won't be possible, because of the danger of a contradiction occurring, but maybe you can find some other slight way, just a tiny tweak, to show him our gratitude …"

Blah blah blah…

"Very well then! Oh, and see if he can be recruited for further missions. He'll get over it. Maybe he'll meet another woman and fall in love again. POSENT can always use a few dedicated agents."

So saying, she rang off without a parting or closing word, in the courtly manner of the Lords of Time Town.

She handed the phone to the maid, who carried the phone back to its cabinet.

Lady Chivet Betize, the Third Postal Lord of Time Town, raised the ornate handle of her binocular opera glasses. She resumed looking through her lens tubes at the Dissolve, noting that the whether-or-not report called for a danger quotient was a Minus {00.89} today. Not bad for a city in perpetual crisis.

She looked pleased with all of her many machinations, and her priorities, and with the progress of the city's warring but patriotic factions in slowly righting the capsized ship of time.

General Tenc Hoseth of the Postal Service, and the cat Donald on his lap, both looked on with satisfaction. They sat looking at another window in the wagon-lit style library, not far from their boss.

A heavy, ornate grandfather clock ticked loudly among the carpets, books, astrolabes, guns, and even more anachronistic and peculiar trophies from the general's many years of service.

The clock emitted a throaty, rich, happy little chime, imitating some long ago church or university clock tower, sending its message across some vanished summer meadow.

Time wasn't what it used to be, but today it was flowing well—at the moment anyway. One must enjoy the little pleasures while they lasted.

"Meow," said Donald.

Dreaming of Carly

16. Dreaming of Carly

Mack felt confused as he staggered out of a sphere of bluish light. He held his head with his hand as he stumbled into a pitch darkness alive with the gibbeting of a thousand frogs.

Hearing a noise behind him, he turned, just in time to see a train start to roll away and a wall replace the station. The light winked out of existence, leaving only the night at Ocotillo Wells and the brown and green spots floating before Mack's eyes.

It took a few minutes for his eyes to get back to normal.

Where am I?

He vaguely remembered this place, but memory was starting to return. For some reason, he'd gotten out of his car and walked to here. He stood looking at a bend in the starlit river. He saw the strong currently flowing quietly between banks of high reeds.

For a moment, he had a strange vision. He saw a white flying machine hovering over the foggy river bend. Indistinct figures were splashing and fighting in the water. A dead woman's lower torso hung from a harness…ghosts…part of a tweak that had to be undone, a change that should not have happened, a skirmish in an eternal time war that must be undone and everything put back the way it had been to avoid a fatal contradiction…

The river looked peaceful, haunted only by the long-dead Native Americans who still walked these valleys at night on their way between the mountains and the sea. The fog slowly moved in swirls, and the current rippled quietly underneath it.

Oh yes. He stooped to pick up his two-foot steel flashlight, which lay near his feet on mossy, damp soil.

He pressed the button and light shot out, illumining a roiling fog all around. Nearly blinded, he shut the light off. He remembered the way he'd come. Walking around a bend, he saw his car. It was a familiar, comforting mass of metal and glass and small parts a few hundred feet ahead.

Something very urgent…but what?

He picked up his steps in the silence of this desert oak grove, a river oasis, and reached the car. He pulled the door open, and the interior dome light shone wanly. Everything was there—his gun lying neatly in a black nylon holster with the black belt wrapped around it. His briefcase was where it should be, as were the reading lamp, and the computer display screen, the radio...There, lying on the console, was a half-eaten tuna fish salad sandwich on white toast, with the edges cut away. He picked it up, smelled it— it was still fresh—and chomped down hungrily. It was delicious and—

The kitchen...

He stopped chewing as it all came back to him. Carly— standing by the island counter, chopping celery to put in his sandwich. Her dark pageboy rocked back and forth as she smiled with nice even teeth and blue eyes. "Hi, honey, I'll have it ready for you in a minute. Don't want my man to starve on the job."

Carly...

He reached in and picked up the microphone. Screw radio silence. "Ten ten base, this is Mack, do you copy—over?"

No response.

He tried several times, without any luck, and thought he must be out of radio range.

At this moment, there were four men savagely beating her, stabbing her, kicking her, all in revenge and hate for being a cop's wife. He jumped into the car, pulled the door shut, started it, and fishtailed down the dirt path, onto the rural road, and on his way to Interstate 8.

He looked at the clock.

Eleven.

Too late.

Why had he not pleaded with Beasley to set it an hour earlier? But Beasley still had him hypnotized and they didn't want him to make a tweak. The big computers uptime had said no to saving Carly. He would find a way. If he had to go uptime and find those bastards and shove his gun down their throats, he would find a way to make them tweak the past.

With the front grill lights flickering madly, and his sirens keening up and down like wounded animals screaming in pain, he went over 100 miles per hour as soon as he reached the Interstate. Nobody was going to interfere with a police car going that fast with full lights and siren. If he were lucky, he might pick up a Highway Patrol car or two for escort. He kept trying the radio, but all he got was interference. Maybe they'd broken off the antenna.

He looked behind him, but it was securely set on the trunk lid, along with other antennas.

He fished around under and around the seat, and found his cell phone. Flicking its clam shell open as he tore along in the left lane, driving all other motorists out of his way, but swerving like a streak around slow moving trucks, he pressed the predial for Home.

The phone rang and rang.

No answer.

Carly, pick up! Pick up! Honey, pick up!

Nothing.

The recording device must be off, maybe torn from the wall, lying on the floor…

He pressed the predial for Leo Roberts, his partner, who'd been delayed getting to the stakeout.

"Mack!" came his partner's voice. "We're on our way out there to look for you. Where have you been? Been trying to call you to let you know the mission got scrubbed."

"Leo, listen. Get to my house as fast as possible. Send black and whites. There are several men in the house, killing Carly."

"Okay! I'm in El Cajon on State 94, and I'll turn around. Can you radio base?"

"Not working. I'm doing 120 here going west on I-8…

"I'll call San Diego PD for you. Hang in there, buddy."

"Thanks." He folded the cell phone shut and put it aside. Everything was a blur around him, almost like the Temporale trains. It wasn't the speed so much as the emotional blender, the fact that he was about to get to his house a few minutes too late, and find her torn to shreds in a mass of gore by those animals…

He slowed down to sixty and took the College Avenue exit, avoiding a line of cars moving so slowly they seemed to be standing still.

He went uphill, past the university, and dove into the mess of tangled little streets in his old neighborhood.

He was the first responder. No other sirens. He shut his lights and sirens off so as not to tip anyone off.

He turned on to his street and cruised quietly to a stop in the middle of the street before his house.

As he got out of the car, gun drawn, and started running, he saw that the lights were all off at the house.

On his left, he saw the headlights and flashers of Leo's green Crown Victoria approaching. The Vic came to a rocking stop, and Leo was out the door holding his Glock in both hands. He was in plainclothes, wearing a dark plaid shirt and corduroy trousers.

At the same time, on his right, he saw Carly sauntering toward him, in the light of street lamps amid the old familiar eucalyptus trees, carrying her purse. She looked perfectly okay, with her page boy hair and her mid-calf dark summer dress swinging happily left and right. "Hi, honey? What's with the gun?" She saw Leo. "What's the excitement?"

"I'll take the house, you get her," Leo said tersely.

Mack ran to his wife and took her in his arm, guiding her quickly to safety behind parked cars across the street. "I am so happy to see you," he told her. Now he really was bawling.

She touched his cheek and looked into his eyes with a worry-face. "Sweetheart—"

At that moment, three San Diego Police black and white patrol cars came tearing up the street from one direction, and another three cruisers came flying down the street from the other direction. They made a mess of screaming sirens and madly flashing lights of all colors. They screeched to a halt before Mack's house. The entire street was illumined like a disco as blue-uniformed police brandishing shotguns poured out and took positions.

Leo stood cautiously to one side on the front porch, out of possible trajectory if there were narco-gangsters inside and they started shooting. Leo waved his badge and called out: "DEA Special Agent. Hold your fire. I'm the caller."

"Where did you go?" Mack pressed her, holding her by the arms with both hands as if to shake her in his worry and frenzy.

"Why," she said, "it was the oddest little thing. I was taking out the trash, and a wind blew the door shut. I had my key in my pocket, so I tried to open the door, but the deadbolt was jammed shut. It looked like someone broke off a key and it was stuck in there and I couldn't get it out. So I finally gave up and went down the street to the Weinbergs to call a locksmith. I got to talking with Jody Weinberg while Simon was looking for a good locksmith who wouldn't charge and arm and a leg. I think I was up there for over an hour. The locksmith should be arriving any time now."

Hearing the sound of his front door being kicked in, Mack turned. A police captain and a sergeant were conferring with Leo, while two brawny policemen with a steel battering ram finished the door off. As the door sagged into the house, a mass of officers moved cautiously into the interior. They went step by step, aiming shotguns, shining flashlights, covering each other.

During a long four or five minutes of silence, two huge red fire engines with throaty sirens keening arrived on the street, the first paramedic responders.

Leo stepped out on the porch, accompanied by the uniformed police supervisor, who called to a sergeant standing on the sidewalk: "All clear. There's a pile of dead guys in the kitchen. There's blood an inch deep on the floor and all over the walls. The furniture is smashed and it looks almost like a grenade went off, or else someone the size of a gorilla went nuts with a machete in each hand. I can't tell what happened. There's nothing but body parts and tattoos. Don't bother with the paramedics nor even with body bags. Just get the M.E. out here with shovels and trashcans."

Mack holstered his weapon and hugged his wife.

Carly wrapped her arms tightly around him. They stood in an aura of shock. He could feel her trembling." Mack, what's going on?"

He squeezed her. "Honey, it's over. All I know is you're alive and well. That's all that matters. You know what?"

She looked up at him with a radiant but apprehensive expression.

"I've decided I'm going to put in the paperwork tomorrow for a desk job. I've done my time in the field."

She laughed and jumped for joy. She threw her arms around him even more tightly. He closed his eyes and buried his face in the fragrance of her neck. He was so glad that she was alive.

That they were both alive.

As he slowly opened his eyes, Mack saw crowds gathering on the sidewalks all around. Among them, he noticed a tallish man with brown hair and rather scary dark eyes. The man wore one of those little forward tilting European fishermen's caps with a snap holding the visor and the front together over the eyes. He stood with his hands in the pockets of his windbreaker, while kicking casually at the ground with toes clad in deck shoes. All very innocent.

Beasley.

The agent from the distant future gave Mack a little wave, and grinned. Beasley held one hand up to show a broken-off key. He'd disobeyed orders, and found just the tiniest of tweaks, a broken key, to show Time Town's gratitude. In the same motion, holding the key, he flicked a casual salute with two fingers against the brim of his hat. He turned and sauntered off, down the street full of twirling lights and squawking radios.

Beasley walked away toward the city lights, noticed only by Mack. He would shortly step through the nearest Temporale portal for his trip home, and the next mission.

Time must flow.

The City of the Universe would be saved—from its broken wreckage on the very shores and reefs of the Cosmopause, from its enemies—and just as much—from its people and their unchanging human nature, the Human Condition.

Easter Egg Brought to You by the Great Shepherd

Thank you Tax Payers and God Bless

Easter Egg Brought to You by the Resistance

Thanks, Losers.

More Info & Titles from Clocktower Books at:

John Argo is a major pseudonym of John T. Cullen, an Active Member of International Thriller Writers (ITW) with over fifty books out (poetry, fiction, nonfiction). He is the publisher of Clocktower Books, a San Diego, California based independent press.

John T. Cullen's webplex (multiple linked author & publisher websites)is anchored at his main site https://www.johntcullen.com.

John Argo has at least seven novels (and some short stories) available in the Empire of Time series at Amazon.com. See:

https://www.amazon.com/John-Argo/e/B00JF9U5XY?ref=dbs_a_def_rwt_hsch_vu00_tkin_p1_i0

or search Amazon.com for "John Argo."

Time Train is Book #4 in the Time Train Series.

John Argo also has numerous other SFFH titles available in the DarkSF series at Amazon as well, in addition to suspense thrillers and romantic novels.

Clocktower Books is a Recognized Publisher of International Thriller Writers (ITW). We have been pioneers in digital and Internet publishing since 1996. More info at the Clocktower Books Museum site:

Readers ask: "So what is DarkSF?" The answer begins with what DarkSF is not. DarkSF is not horror, gruesome, juvenile, or slasher fare. Dark does not mean scary, Rather, we like to say that "DarkSF is the dark chocolate of Speculative Fiction."

DarkSF is richly textured, literate, first-class science fiction in the tradition best explained by comparing with classic, artistic films like Blade Runner (1982 dir. Ridley Scott); Dark City (1998 dir. Alex Proyas); The Matrix (1999 dir. Wachowskis); or Chrysalis (2007 dir. Julien Leclercq) to name just a few of the best. More Info:

https://www.empireoftime.com/, https://www.darksf.com, or https://www.fictiongenres.com/.

www.ingramcontent.com/pod-product-compliance
Lightning Source LLC
Chambersburg PA
CBHW031833170626
46807CB00004B/1445